We stared wide-eyed at the gray-and-white running shoe protruding from the chicory and wild phlox lining the path.

My pulse accelerated to a rate that far outstripped the hammering I'd experienced when jogging. *Oh, God,* I prayed, unable to articulate all the thoughts that raced through my mind. *I don't want to look. I must look. What should I do if she needs help?* If *she needs help? Of course she needs help. She's lying on the ground, and I doubt she's just taking a nap.*

Carefully I leaned over the weeds, following the line of the woman's body, for it was obvious from the size of her foot and the shape of her ankle that it was a woman. She was lying on her stomach, face turned toward the left, away from us, sleeveless pink scoop-necked knit shirt twisted about her torso.

It was the wound at the back of her head and the trampled weeds surrounding her that made my stomach tighten.

Books by Gayle Roper

Steeple Hill Women's Fiction

See No Evil #39
Caught in the Middle #50
Caught in the Act #54
Caught in a Bind #58
Caught Redhanded #64

GAYLE ROPER

has always loved stories, and she's authored forty books of her own. Gayle has won Romance Writers of America's RITA® Award for Best Inspirational Romance, finaled repeatedly for both a RITA® Award and a Christy® Award, won three Holt Medallions, a Reviewers' Choice Award, an Inspirational Readers Choice Contest and a Lifetime Achievement Award, as well as an Award of Excellence. Several writers' conferences have cited her for her contributions to the training of writers. Her articles have appeared in numerous periodicals, including *Discipleship Journal* and *Moody Magazine,* and she has contributed chapters and short stories to several anthologies. She enjoys speaking at writers' conferences and women's events, reading and eating out. She adores her kids and grandkids, and loves her own personal patron of the arts, her husband, Chuck.

GAYLE ROPER

CAUGHT REDHANDED

Published by Steeple Hill Books™

STEEPLE HILL BOOKS

ISBN-13: 978-0-373-44254-6
ISBN-10: 0-373-44254-8

CAUGHT REDHANDED

This edition published by arrangement with Steeple Hill Books.

www.SteepleHill.com

Printed in U.S.A.

And the Lord said to [Moses],
"What is that in your hand?"
—*Exodus* 4:2

Who will ascend to the hill of the Lord?
Who will stand in his holy place?
Those who have clean hands and a pure heart…
—*Psalms* 24:3–4

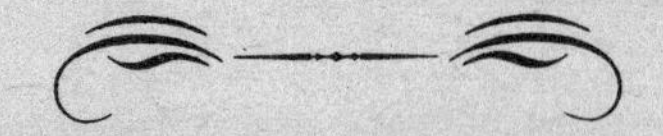

To Chip and Audrey

and

Jeff and Cindy,

we couldn't be prouder.

Acknowledgments

Thanks to Jim Ford, director,
Good Works of Chester County, PA,
for taking time to talk with me.
You and the hundreds who help you
have put that which God has put in
your hand to service for the King.
I appreciate you and all the others.

ONE

"I need to get in shape," I said one mid-July day as I sat at my desk at *The News: The Voice of Amhearst and Chester County* where I was a general reporter. "For the wedding."

My wedding was less than two weeks away and I knew that realistically not much could change in that short a time. It was more a case of hope springing eternal. After all, if the women's magazines could guarantee the loss of a bagillion pounds in one week, why shouldn't I lose a few by exercising a time or two before I said "I do"?

Still, I didn't mean for anyone to take me up on the comment, certainly not for anyone to challenge me to actually do something about it. It was more one of those rhetorical statements I tend to make, and I neither expect nor want a response.

"You need to take up jogging." Jolene Marie Luray Meister Samson looked me up and down from her desk across the aisle. "You could use it."

Just because she was beautiful and had a figure to

die for was no reason to give me that condescending look. I might not be up to her standard of pulchritude, but I was hardly ugly. Curt, my one true love, seemed satisfied, and what more did I need?

"Thanks, Jo," I said dryly. "Just the encouragement I need."

She nodded, taking my words at face value. "I'll meet you in the parking lot at Bushay's tomorrow morning at six-thirty. It's still cool enough to run at that hour. We'll take the jogging trail they have through the woods. It's pretty, too. Goes beside a creek part of the way and through the woods the rest of the way."

I'm pretty sure my mouth dropped open, making me look addlepated. I couldn't decide which threw me more, the hour for the suggested run or the fact that Jolene seemed to be saying she jogged. I wouldn't have expected one scintilla of physical exertion from her, not even running for her life. And I was supposed to believe she jogged regularly?

"What?" she asked, somewhat huffily. "You think I got this figure by praying for it? I jog three or four times a week."

"Even in winter?" I was overwhelmed at the picture of Jolene in sweats and watch cap, breath pluming behind her.

"Then I use the track at the Y."

"At 6:30 a.m.?" Edie Whatley stared. She was the editor of our family page and a general reporter, a slightly plump, happily married woman with a sixteen-year-old son. She looked as shocked as I did at the twin thoughts of Jolene jogging and the hour.

"What is the matter with you two?" Jolene demanded, allowing a frown to mar her lovely face. "Just because you always see me when I'm beautiful..."

She let her voice die, but not because she was embarrassed to have called herself beautiful. She was a strong proponent of truth in advertising, even when it was self-promotion. Rather, she'd just had an idea. I could tell because she narrowed her eyes as she looked from me to Edie and back. The newsroom at *The News* was small and looking from desk to desk was not in the least difficult.

"I dare you both," she said. "I dare you to run with me. Prove you've got the guts and the stamina."

Edie and I looked at each other with more than a touch of disbelief.

"You've got to stay looking good for Tom, Edie. And you—" Jolene pointed at me with one of her lethal fingernails "—you need to keep Curt interested. You're not married yet."

But soon, I thought joyfully. *Soon.*

"Is that how you keep Reilly interested?" I asked, not willing to tell her that I didn't think a few pounds one way or the other would make Curt lose or gain interest. He was too much a man of principle to be repelled by something as petty as a few pounds. Not that I planned on gaining any weight, but I was wise enough to know that life happened. After all, Mom had once been a size ten.

"Jolene," Edie said kindly, "Tom is fine with me the way I am, just as I'm sure Reilly loves you just the way you are."

Jolene grinned at the mention of her husband to whom she had now been married for several months.

"And I must tell you," Edie continued, "that I gave up dares in junior high school."

"Just because you're well past junior high doesn't mean you can't accept a challenge," Jolene said, either unaware or uncaring that she had just semi-insulted Edie.

"Look, kiddo." Edie emphasized the *kid* in *kiddo*. Jolene was about my age, which was just-turned twenty-seven. "No jogging. I exercise enough to feel healthy and that's all I plan to do."

I nodded, though I didn't get any more exercise than running from story to story.

"You're afraid," Jolene taunted, her eyes on me. Apparently she recognized Edie as a lost cause.

"Get real."

"You know I'll whip you frontward and backward."

"I doubt that."

"Tomorrow morning," Jo said. "Six-thirty. I'll be waiting."

And that's how I ended up winded, trying my best to keep up with the lovely Jolene, who was proving herself a more than capable jogger as we traced the trail through the woods behind Bushay Waste Management. She wasn't even huffing in her Lycra top and jogging shorts, her perfect, long legs eating up the distance, her iPod clipped to her waistband, the wire to her earbuds swaying with each stride.

I, on the other hand, expected to fall over any

moment. My feet had never felt so heavy, my legs so much like jelly. I pressed my hand against the pain spearing my side.

"Wait for me!" I managed to get the words out between puffs. Why I ever thought this romp in the woods would be a snap was beyond me. You'd think I'd have learned by now that just because Jo looked like a piece of beautiful fluff didn't mean she was one. Edie had warned me often enough.

Even yesterday after I'd fallen into Jo's trap, she'd said, "Merry, Jo never speaks from a position of weakness. If she thought she'd lose this dare, she'd never have made it."

I'd waved her wise words away, but I should have listened, especially since Jo sat at her desk with that cat-who-ate-the-canary look of smug satisfaction.

Even Curt cautioned me when he called to say goodnight. "Don't be too cocky, sweetheart. Jolene likes to win. Always."

"Yeah, yeah," I muttered, not the least bit concerned.

Now I was just hoping to make it back to the parking lot without totally embarrassing myself because it was a given that Jo would never let me forget if I failed.

The early morning humidity made everything blur around the edges as I ran. At least I thought it was the humidity and not failing eyesight due to physical overexertion. I tried to ignore the pains shooting through my shins at every step.

"Slacker," Jolene yelled back at me over her shoulder.

And that moment of inattention to the path threw us both into the middle of another murder.

I watched in horror as Jolene tripped and went down flat.

"Jo!" I forced myself to go a bit faster. "Are you all right?"

Now she was gasping, too, the wind knocked out of her. "Fine," she managed in a raspy voice as I knelt beside her.

She pushed herself onto her hands and knees, still struggling for oxygen, head hanging. Bracing herself on one arm, she held out the other scraped and bleeding palm. We inspected it carefully. She turned it over and breathed a sigh of relief. "No broken nails."

I'd been more concerned about broken limbs.

She sank back on her heels and held out her other palm. Scraped and slowly oozing blood, too. She flipped the hand over. A broken nail, the middle finger. She said a few of the words that Edie and I were trying to convince her weren't ladylike. Obviously we had more work to do.

She climbed slowly to her feet, looking down at her knees. More oozing scrapes.

"Now how am I supposed to wear skirts with scabs all over my legs?" she demanded.

"Wear pants," I said with an appalling lack of sympathy. Now that I knew she was all right, I was back to being disgruntled.

She gave her typical snort, always so surprising from someone who looks like her. Clearly she felt a mandate to share her beautiful limbs with the world. How she had become one of my best friends was still a mystery to me. She was even going to be one of my bridesmaids along with Maddie and Dawn.

"I tripped over something." Jo sounded as if whatever she had stumbled over had deliberately attacked her. She pushed to her feet with me helping by taking her elbow.

We turned together to see what had brought her low and stared wide eyed at the foot clad in a gray-and-white running shoe protruding from the chicory and wild phlox lining the path.

My pulse accelerated to a rate that far outstripped the hammering I'd experienced when jogging. *Oh, God,* I prayed, unable to articulate all the thoughts that raced through my mind. *I don't want to look. I must look. What should I do if she needs help?* If *she needs help? Of course she needs help. She's lying on the ground and I doubt she's just taking a nap.*

Carefully I leaned over the weeds, following the line of the woman's body, for it was obvious from the size of her foot and the shape of her ankle that it was a woman. She was lying on her stomach, face turned toward the left, away from us, sleeveless pink scoop-necked knit shirt twisted about her torso.

It was the gaping wound at the back of her head and the bloody weeds surrounding her that made my stomach heave.

TWO

I swallowed and then swallowed some more until the urge to be sick subsided.

"Martha!" Jolene said in a disbelieving voice. "It's Martha Colby!"

I might have known she'd recognize the woman. Jo has lived in Amhearst all her life and knows everyone who lives here—and all their secrets.

I knelt quickly beside Martha, taking care not to step in the blood, and felt for a pulse. As I looked into her open, staring eyes, I didn't expect to find one. I didn't. I glanced at Jo and saw she had lost all her color and was swaying slightly. I understood completely. If I felt this shaky and I didn't even know the woman, how must Jo feel?

"Why don't you run for help?" I suggested quickly. Neither of us had carried our cells as we ran, but mostly I wanted to get her out of here before she passed out.

"911," she said vaguely.

"911," I agreed. "I'll stay here with Martha."

Jo blinked at me, nodded, then took off, running

with remarkable speed. I felt a maternal pride—or what I think such a thing feels like—in her quick reaction. The last time we faced a body together, she'd fallen to pieces. Of course, it had been her ex-husband's body then.

I sat down beside Martha's foot on the path. She looked so vulnerable, so sad lying there. So alone. For some reason I wanted to rest my hand on her foot, on her running shoe. I fought the feeling that she needed attachment, touch, because she no longer did. I was the one who did. Death always brings home the fragility of life.

But if I touched her anywhere, even if I only touched her shoe, I might inadvertently destroy evidence. Who knew what she might have stepped in and what trace evidence lingered on that surface?

I blinked as I realized I was assuming murder. Why?

My eyes swept over the area. There was no limb lying nearby that might have fallen on her. In fact, there were no trees close to the path where we were. Also Martha couldn't have stumbled and struck the back of her head, nor could the soft earth beneath the chicory and phlox and wild mustard have made that horrid gash.

The scene said foul play as clearly as if the weeds themselves could speak.

So I sat by Martha's foot, careful not to touch her, feeling she deserved someone acting as honor guard or some such thing, though we were obviously too late to shield her from whomever had harmed her.

Suddenly it struck me that her neck had still been warm when I felt for a pulse. My back muscles contracted as I quickly scanned the edge of the woods that stood back about twenty feet from the trail. Dogwood and mountain laurel, their blossoms now gone, mixed with poplar, beech and oak. Whoever had struck Martha might still be nearby. Maybe they were watching me from behind the thicket of bushes? The summer foliage was dense enough to hide a small army if it chose to secret itself behind the trees. Certainly one murderer could be hiding there easily.

Oh, Lord, if he's there, make him go away! I remembered my manners and quickly added, *Please!*

"They're on their way," Jo called as she raced back.

I breathed a relieved sigh. Help was coming and there was safety in numbers, even if the number was only two at the moment.

Jo shoved her picture phone at me. "Here, take a few shots before the crime-scene guys arrive and we won't be allowed near Martha again."

"I hate this part of being a reporter." I climbed to my feet and took the phone.

"Mac would kill us if we missed the opportunity." She heard herself and made a distressed noise as she looked down at Martha. "Poor choice of words."

"Yeah." Trying to be the uninvolved newspaper professional, I took several pictures. When the police arrived, I'd take a couple more of them at work and it would be one of those that actually got printed in the paper. We certainly wouldn't print Martha, so defenseless, lying here. The pain that would give her family was unimaginable. But we would use them as a reference for whatever we wrote.

Jo stayed carefully on the path, but continued to

stare at Martha, looking sad. "I went to school with her younger sister Tawny."

"Tawny? Like the color of a lion?" It's amazing the strange things your mind sticks on when reality is too terrible to contemplate.

"Yeah."

"Interesting. Martha is such a traditional name, biblical and all. Tawny is one of those cutesy modern names."

"Different moms. Martha's mom took off when she was about three. Left her with her father. He remarried a couple of years later, and Tawny and Shawna come from the second marriage. Martha was four or five years ahead of Tawny and me, but I always thought she was so cool. She was a cheerleader, the real perky kind who does splits and tumbles. Mac was her tosser."

"Mac?" I squeaked. "Our Mac?"

Mac Carnuccio was our editor at *The News,* and he was also Amhearst born and bred. He might be many things, but I'd never in a million years have pictured him as a cheerleader. The secrets that lurk in people's pasts are amazing.

Jolene nodded. "Our Mac. He and Martha went together from high school until well into college. Then when he came back to town to work at *The News,* they dated again, sort of off and on when he wasn't chasing someone else. He sort of broke her heart."

That sounded like our Mac.

Jo shrugged and looked thoughtful, always a circumstance guaranteed to bring an unexpected insight. "Or maybe she broke his. Who knows? She dated other guys a lot."

Now there was an interesting thought. Mac, a ladies' man through and through, reaping his own whirlwind.

"And in a fit of frustrated passion—" she waved her arm in the air like she was banging something against the back of a head "—he…"

I frowned at her. "Don't even go there, Jolene Marie. You know Mac is changing. And even the old Mac would never have done something so violent."

Jo actually blushed. "Yeah, you're right." She leaned over Martha, I thought because she was too embarrassed to look at me. Accusing one's boss, even in thoughtless speculation, isn't the done thing.

Jo tensed. "Look. She's got a tattoo on her left shoulder."

I looked. Sure enough, sticking out from under the edge of her sleeveless running shirt was the curve of one side of a red heart.

"It has a name in it," Jo said. Before I realized what she planned to do, she reached over and slid the shirt to the side.

"Jo! Don't touch!" I could picture the unhappy face of Sergeant Poole of the Amhearst police.

Jolene ignored me just as she ignored anything she didn't want to hear. "It says *M-A-C. MAC.*" She looked at me. "Our Mac?"

Yikes. The very thought made me uneasy.

"Even if it is, it doesn't mean anything anymore," Jolene hastened to say, obviously trying to undo her previous suspicious thoughts. "He's going with Dawn Trauber now."

He wishes. Dawn was the director of His House, a

residential ministry to teen girls in trouble, most of them unwed mothers. She was also a strong Christian and Mac wasn't. I didn't think he was any kind of a believer, strong or weak, committed or un. Therein lay their problem. In spite of mutual attraction, Dawn was holding tough against too deep an emotional attachment. At least she was trying hard. It was a case of unequally yoked.

"It looks new, doesn't it?" Jo asked, still studying the tattoo.

I knew nothing about tattoos except that they were permanent and that it hurt to get them. Oh, and that as you aged and your skin sagged, so did your tattoo.

The first response team arrived in an amazingly short time, swarming the area, cordoning off the crime scene with yellow tape. My friend Sergeant William Poole led the police contingent.

"What is it with you two?" he asked, his furrowed face curious as he studied Jo and me. "You turn up at an inordinate number of homicides, especially you, Merry."

I gave him a sickly grin. "You think I enjoy it?"

He smiled kindly, his furrowed face wrinkling like a shar-pei's. "Of course you don't, any more than I do." His eyes took on a teasing glint. "But I think you love the stories."

I couldn't deny that, ghoulish as it made me seem. For a reporter everything is a potential story and bombshells like local murders are guaranteed to interest readers. I looked at the crime-scene investigators hovering over Martha. "The stories may be great,

William, but I'd rather not have them. They hurt too many people."

I thought of Martha's family. Were her father and stepmother about to be devastated? Or wouldn't they care? Did she have more siblings than Tawny and Shawna, perhaps ones who shared the same mother? Had Martha been close to her much younger half sisters? Where was her mother now? Had Martha had contact with her or had she disappeared completely from her daughter's life?

Oh, Lord, they're all going to need your comfort. Be there for them.

William nodded. "This one definitely hurts. I watched her grow up." He sighed. "Her family lives down the street from us."

"What kind of a young woman was she?" I asked. There I went, story-writing again.

"Most of the time she was great. When she was in high school, she babysat for our kids. At college she went a little wild for a time—a couple of DUIs, a bust for pot—but she straightened herself out."

"Did she still live at home?"

"No." He and Jolene said it together.

"She had her own place," William said.

"Over in those new condos off Chestnut Street," Jolene said.

I knew the condos she meant. They were nice, moderately priced units, built about four years ago. They didn't begin to compare with the luxury condo that Jolene shared with Reilly, but then, not many did. Not many people had an income like Jolene's. Twenty-five thousand dollars a month for twenty years. She and her late husband, Arnie, had hit it big in the state lottery.

"Did she live alone?"

Jo shook her head. "Her latest boyfriend is Ken Mackey. They share."

"Mackey?" William cast an unhappy eye in her direction.

Jo nodded but for once kept her mouth shut. Hmm. Definitely something to be learned there. Between Jo's silence and the way William said Ken Mackey's name, we had an issue with a capital *I*. When Jo and I were in the office, I'd nail her for the scoop on old Ken.

"You two can go home and get ready for work," William said. "Just stop at the station today and give a formal statement. If I'm not there, ask for Officer Schumann."

We nodded and turned to leave. I paused and took a few shots of the men and women working the scene. William saw me and gave me an unhappy look, but he didn't forbid me. I appreciated his trust.

Poor Martha appeared to have trusted the wrong person.

THREE

As William suggested, I went home and showered. I ran my mousse-globbed hands through my hair, trying to make it look stylishly spiked instead of like I hadn't bothered to brush it today. I put on navy slacks, a pink wide-strapped camisole top and a white sheer blouse covered with pink flowers. I liked the way the pink in the cami made the pink flowers in the sheer blouse so vivid. And I immediately felt guilty for thinking about something so frivolous with Martha lying dead.

With a sigh I snuggled Whiskers, my much-pampered cat, for a moment, then went to the kitchen. I kept one eye on the clock as I toasted a couple of slices of Jewish rye nice and crisp. I slathered them lavishly with real butter and ate them with a Diet Coke as I drove to the office, all too aware that deadline was looming. I needed to do my piece on Martha.

This wasn't the first time I'd written about a crime with which I was intimately connected and I disliked it this time just as much as the first time I'd inadvertently found death. My heart bled for the lost life, for the lost opportunities, the lost joys and sorrows, and most deeply for the lost chances to know God intimately. My soul shriveled at the audacity of someone who thought that the right to decide life and death was his. How heinous, how prideful, how offensive. How evil. It was Cain and Abel wearing modern garb, man killing man for power and greed, love and hate. It was proof positive that mankind had not changed though we dressed better and enjoyed luxuries those biblical brothers could not even imagine.

And there were those left behind who through no choice of their own were forced to share Eve's sorrow and loss, compelled to forfeit part of their lives, too. I'd seen their faces and their pain. I'd written about it, attempted to comprehend their great bereavement and make readers feel it and understand that as the victim had been robbed of so many possibilities, so had those who loved that person.

I wanted to be a voice for the dead and for those they left behind, to articulate their horror, their despair. If in this way I could make some contribution to the apprehension of the person responsible for all this pain, I would feel I had offered some small compensation to those who remained.

Chin up, shoulders back, I marched into the newsroom, Joan of Arc to my own fields of Orléans.

"How many inches?" I called to Mac, the can of Coke still in my hand. I swallowed the dregs as he called back, "As much as you need. We'll adapt."

I stared. I wasn't used to such freedom and it felt strange.

Mac scowled at me. "Just write, Kramer. Fast."

I blinked. "Right."

I wrote a straight news piece, not too long since the incident was only an hour or so old and neither I nor the police had had time to gather much information. Then I wrote the personal piece, adding quotes from Jolene to flesh it out, trying my best to communicate the horror without titillating. I dragged the icon for the pieces and dropped them into Mac's in-box, then sat back in my chair and thought about the morning. I got up abruptly. I wanted to go to the crime scene and see firsthand if anything new and interesting had developed.

I parked in the Bushay lot, now full of cars. Most were those of employees, but several had flashing lights and crackling radios. I followed the jogging path to the yellow crime-scene tape. Sergeant Poole looked up from his blue study of the matted grass where Martha had lain. He stood alone, but clever sleuth that I am, I knew there were other cops somewhere because of the cars in the lot.

William's craggy face grew ever more furrowed as he frowned at me. "Merry."

I decided to ignore the lack of enthusiasm in his voice. "Hi, William. Anything new happening?"

He extended his arm to indicate the empty space around him. "As you can see, not a thing."

"Any comment for the paper? What have the crime-scene guys found?"

"The investigation is continuing apace."

I cocked an eyebrow at him. He was the only person I knew who said *apace*.

"Sorry, kid," he said, not sorry at all. "That's it."

"No weapon? No motive? No suspect?"

"Merry, the woman's been dead mere hours."

"Hey, William! Come 'ere quick!"

He and I turned to the woman who burst out of the woods, ducking under the graceful branches of a dogwood. She wore a uniform like William's without the stripes of rank. Her face was alight with excitement.

"Oops." Officer Natalie Schumann skidded to a halt as she saw me. "Uh, Sergeant Poole, may I see you for a moment, please?"

"If you'll excuse me, Merry," William said. "I'm sure you need to leave and get about your reporting business somewhere else. Maybe there's a fire in West Chester or a drug bust in Downingtown." He nodded and turned to follow Natalie into the woods.

As soon as William and Natalie disappeared into the trees, I followed as quietly as I could. At times like this I find it wonderful that my work provides me a legitimate excuse for my nosiness. No guilt for a change.

About a football field into the woods I saw a cluster of cops standing around what appeared to be a large thicket of raspberry brambles growing in a patch of sunlight. One of the men was picking ripe berries and popping them in his mouth as he and the others watched someone in the middle of the thicket intently.

That officer was taking pictures of something from all angles. He muttered words that I would never say as thorns tore at his uncovered arms and clung to his uniform pants. His particularly loud snarls seemed reserved for the ripe raspberries that insisted on bleeding all over him.

I snuck up behind Natalie and tried to peer around her. I needed to see what had attracted all this attention. When I couldn't see as well as I wanted, I stepped forward and trod on a rock hidden under the natural refuse littering the ground. My ankle turned and with a squeak I pitched forward into the raspberries. Normally I love the wild raspberries that grow profusely on fences and stone walls at the edge of fields as well as in clusters like this where sunlight penetrates the canopy of leaves. The early flowers smell spicy with a hint of cinnamon and I enjoy picking the fruit when it ripens. However, falling into a thicket is a different matter.

I threw my hands out as if they would protect me. It raced through my mind that the scratches I was sure to get should clear up before the wedding. Unless they festered.

Just before I went in headfirst, a strong arm grabbed my blouse in the back and pulled me up short. When I got my feet under me, I glanced over my shoulder at William.

"I thought I told you to get lost," he growled.

Ever astute, I deduced that he was not happy to see me. Ignoring his comment, I smiled at him. "Thank you, William," I said most sincerely. "The bride wore scratches isn't the look I want. What are you all looking at?"

It was obvious he didn't want to tell me, but at that moment the cop emerged from the grasp of the raspberry brambles, still muttering under his breath as he tried to detach one long tendril that insisted on clinging to his pants. His arms were laced with red scratches and berry stains. His light blue shirt would be a total loss if the red polka dots stained as I thought they would.

William forgot me as he stepped close to examine what the cop held balanced on a piece of toweling.

"Paper bag," William called and Natalie flipped open what looked like a bag from the grocery store. Carefully the officer from the raspberries slid his find into the bag—a jagged rock large enough to be a deadly weapon, a rock stained with blood, a rock that had strands of hair stuck to it.

My stomach churned as I pictured the murderer bringing it down on the head of an unsuspecting Martha.

"Natalie, take it to the crime-scene guys at the Lancaster barracks," William ordered.

With a brisk nod, she and her paper bag were gone.

"Why a paper bag?" I asked William. On TV they always use plastic bags.

"So moisture doesn't build up inside and break down the chemical properties of the blood and the other trace elements."

"I'm assuming that's the murder weapon?" I indicated Natalie's retreating form.

"I don't know."

"But the blood and hair—"

"We don't know that they belong to the vic." He stared at me. "Goodbye, Merry. I have work to do."

He turned to the officer with the camera and he and the others made a circle that shut me out. And rightly so, I admitted. It was time for me to go.

As I walked to the car, I knew that rock was the

murder weapon just as I knew the blood and hair were Martha's. Otherwise it was a case of one deer walloping another and tossing the rock in the raspberries where he knew it would be hard to find.

Right.

I climbed into my car, lowered the windows to release the heat that had built up and pulled out of my pocket the slip of paper I'd written Martha's address on. I pushed the air-conditioning button and drove across town to her condo development with the windows open. My father would think I was crazy for having the windows open with the air-conditioning going, but I find the resulting mixed temperature most comfortable. I also love the air blowing my hair, which couldn't get too messed up with all the mousse in it.

I wandered up and down the twisting streets west of Amhearst near Sadsburyville for a good five minutes looking for the right road and house number. I became totally confused and began to fear I'd never find my way back out, let alone Martha's place. Why couldn't developers put in straight streets anymore? Life had been so much easier when the line from point A to point B was a straight one instead of a corkscrew. Mazes might be fun to solve on paper or in an autumn cornfield, but in developments they leave a lot to be desired.

Finally I stumbled across the right road and followed the numbers until I came to the series of five attached units, the second from the left being Martha's. Her unit had creamy vinyl siding, crimson shutters and a crimson front door behind a white screen door. The neighboring units were taupe, white, blue and brick. I liked the brick unit best; it had character. But architectural detail wasn't why I was here. I wanted to see if I could find Ken Mackey. Ken MACkey.

I walked to the front door of Martha's condo, noting that only her name, not Ken's, was on the mailbox. A white plastic basket filled with deep red petunias and blue lobelia hung from one corner of the small roof overhanging the front door. In a little patch of soil beside the concrete slab front stoop grew pink geraniums backed by blue salvia and fronted by white alyssum. My heart contracted at the signs of the care Martha had taken to turn her rather ordinary residence into her unique home.

I pushed on the doorbell to the right of the jamb but heard no answering ring. I frowned and pushed again. No trill. I pulled the screen door open and knocked.

And took a step backward as the door swung inward at my touch.

FOUR

I stared at Martha's front door as it slowly creaked open. Not good.

"Hello?" I called into the shadowed front hall. "Is anyone home? Ken?" I knocked on the doorjamb. "Hello?"

I thought maybe I heard a quiet thud and a soft swish. My heart began beating so hard my ears rang. Someone was here. I swallowed and elbowed the door farther open.

"Hello?"

No answer.

Remembering William's edict that I never touch anything at a crime scene—and it didn't take many brains to figure that with the condo's resident dead and the front door unaccountably open, this was probably a crime scene—I didn't touch the knob in case the cops needed to check it for prints or something.

I supposed it was possible that Martha had hurried out this morning to go on her run without shutting and locking her door, but I doubted it. Even I, Merry the

Forgetful, remembered to lock my front door. Not the car necessarily, but definitely the front door.

If Ken was still home, maybe she wouldn't have locked up, but she'd have at least closed the door. I became certain of that as air-conditioned air swirled out of the opening to cool my face. No one was foolish enough to leave a door open with the air-conditioning on at this time of year. I pulled out my cell to call William.

"Martha's not here," said a voice behind me. "She's at work down at the supermarket. You'd think people would realize that at ten-thirty on a Tuesday morning."

I spun and found myself facing a stooped woman with the black hair of a bad home dye-job. Her blue eyes were bright in her wrinkled face and I guessed she was eighty if she was a day. As she gestured toward the house with her chin, her wattles swung gently.

"I guess you've got a key?" She gestured at the open door. "The others had one, too. They said Martha was going to meet them here, but they didn't wait for her very long. When they left, they went out by the back door, sort of sneakylike if you ask me."

They? "Who went out the back? Ken?" Maybe he didn't want to see anyone in his grief. Or if he was guilty, maybe he was grabbing his stuff and getting out while the getting was good. Maybe he thought I was the police.

She nodded her head vigorously and her hair moved not one millimeter. "Ken was first. Then the new boyfriend."

"The new boyfriend?" What new boyfriend? I couldn't believe I was learning something Jolene had missed. "Ken's no longer Martha's boyfriend?"

The woman bent and twisted a dying flower from one of Martha's geraniums. She straightened slowly, vertebra by vertebra. "Not for a couple of months. Good riddance, I say. Hated his motorcycle." She curled her lip. "Loud, smelly thing."

I smiled. "Motorcycles can certainly be loud."

"Not the bike. Him." She gave a sniff. "He was loud and smelly. Never could figure out why she let him stay with her."

I decided I liked Martha's neighbor. "So this is Martha's condo, not Ken's?"

"Oh, yes. Before he came, she lived here alone. Then after he moved out, she lived here alone. The new boyfriend doesn't live with her."

"Who's the new boyfriend?"

"Don't know his name. Tall, but then everyone looks tall to me. Very handsome, at least what I can see of him. He always comes late and I don't see as well as I used to at night or even at twilight. He always wears a cap with some logo on it. I looked at it through my binoculars once." She made a face. "Oops. You didn't hear that, now, did you, dear?"

I laughed. "I didn't hear a thing. Did you figure out what the logo was?"

"It was a bird."

"A bird? Like he was wearing an Eagles cap? Was it dark green and white?"

She thought for a minute. "It could have been dark green. It was certainly dark in color. But the bird didn't look like any eagle I ever saw, but then, what do I know of logos? One thing I will say for the guy, though—he is always very polite. Nods to me whenever he comes. Makes Ken look like a Neanderthal. He never paid any attention to me." She pointed proudly to the baby-blue unit next door. "I live right there."

"Very nice," I said as I looked at the big pot of yellow daisies and blue lobelia on her doorstep. I could see the lace curtains covering her front windows were parted a couple of inches in the center. The better to use those binoculars?

She frowned thoughtfully. "Though come to think of it, I never saw the new one come in the daytime before today. You'd think he'd know Martha's at work."

I looked at the woman, who obviously didn't yet know about Martha's death. I decided not to tell her. I'd been through enough emotional drama and I had no desire to face more. Besides, she might be more open and spontaneous this way, telling me things I wanted to know. I stuck out my hand. "I'm Merry Kramer."

"I'm Doris Wilson, dear. Nice to meet you." She smiled happily as she took my hand. Her gnarled fingers gripped more strongly than I expected.

"Was Martha a good neighbor?" I asked, then kicked myself for using the past tense. I peered at Mrs. Wilson. Maybe she wouldn't catch it.

"Was? Oh dear. Are you telling me she's moving? When Ken left, I thought she might move to get away from the memories, you know? Then she didn't and I thought she was going to stay." Mrs. Wilson sighed. "The nice ones always leave. Sergeant Major Wilson was in the army for many, many years and the nice ones always got reassigned just when we got to know and enjoy them. Or we got reassigned. Are you a real estate lady come to check over the place?"

"No, no, not at all," I hastened to assure her. "I was just asking a question."

Mrs. Wilson absently twisted her wedding ring around her finger. "She's a very nice person. Smokes like a lot of foolish young people, but she's nice. She never hesitates to come over if I need help with something like climbing on the step stool to get a special dish off a high shelf. Oh my." She looked distressed. "If Martha moves, I would be very sad."

A faint ringing sounded and Mrs. Wilson went on point like a bird dog taking the scent. Her nose actually quivered. "That's my phone." She turned eagerly toward her unit. "Nice to meet you, uh—" She gave up trying to recall my name. "I'm sorry Martha's not home."

As soon as her white door closed behind her, I elbowed Martha's door all the way open. In spite of Mrs. Wilson's assurances that "they" went out the back door, I called, "Hello? Hello? I'm coming in."

And I did, pushing the door not quite shut behind me so I could make a quick exit if I needed to. I paused in the hall, listening. The house had that empty feel to it and I decided it was quite safe to look around a bit.

I could just imagine Curt's reaction if he'd been here. "Merry, what are you doing? This isn't your house. You can't just walk in."

Then there was Mac's way of seeing things. I knew he'd say, "Good initiative, Kramer. I'm proud of you. What'd you find?"

As to William, I didn't think he'd see my walk-through as breaking and entering. I wouldn't touch anything and I certainly wouldn't take anything.

All in all, I felt good to go.

Martha's living room looked like it came from an IKEA catalogue, all blond wood and bright cushions. Several inexpensive but attractive framed posters of colorful gardens hung on two of the walls; a flat-screen TV hung on a third over a long entertainment center. Two tall windows looked out on the small front lawn and the parking lot, filling the fourth wall.

Cat stuff was everywhere—pillows sporting cats lined the sofa, two stuffed cats sat in one of the chairs, ceramic cats sat on end tables amid framed photos, a calico fabric cat lay beside the magazine basket. And when I glanced at the gardens on the wall again, I saw they all had cats sitting among the blooms.

I made a mental note to ask Mrs. Wilson if Martha had a live cat or two who needed care now that their owner was dead.

The only jarring note in the room was the disarrangement of the cats and the framed photos that sat in groups on the end tables and the top of the entertainment cabinet. Martha smiled out of several pictures, standing arm in arm with people I didn't know. In three of the many pictures the same young man stood with Martha, his arms wrapped around her. Ken? If so, he didn't look dirty or smelly to me. In fact, he looked pretty good to me. An adorable little girl with blond ringlets grinned from a frame that had been knocked over. A niece? A friend's child? A couple who must be her father and stepmother sat in a rather rigid studio portrait. Beside them a ceramic cat that was washing an extended back leg lay toppled on its side.

On the floor, beside a stone cat sitting with his tail curled about his paws, lay a picture, facedown. Much as I was dying to see the photo since you never know what might be a clue, I didn't touch it. I hoped William would appreciate my discipline.

In the neat, white kitchen a copy of today's *Philadelphia Inquirer* lay on the table, opened to the puzzle page. Someone had begun working the Sudoku with a mechanical pencil that had a very worn eraser. The only other item not tucked away in a cupboard was a small glass with orange juice residue in the bottom. The back sliding glass door stood open, the screen pushed to the side.

Can you say escape route? I was willing to bet this was the swishing sound I'd heard when I first arrived. I gave a little shudder. I had scared someone off, someone I was very glad I hadn't met, given today's circumstances.

I peeked in the single bedroom where a faux brass bed stood, neatly made and covered with an Amish quilt in shades of blue and yellow. Blue and yellow curtains hung at the windows and once again everything was neat as could be—except for the night table whose drawer was wide open. An alarm clock and a book lay on the floor beside the toppled bedside lamp.

I looked in the bathroom last and there the mess left no doubt that someone had taken things or at the very least been looking for something specific. The medicine chest had been emptied into the sink, its door left gaping. Bottles, toiletries and a box of bandages lay in a heap; the toothbrush holder lay on the floor.

I wondered which one of Mrs. Wilson's *they* had made the mess.

I went back to the kitchen and stared at the open sliding door. Hot, humid air poured in, melding with the crisp air-conditioning. The view out the door was the backs of another five-condo unit, separated from Martha's by a row of conifers that had grown both tall and thick. I wondered if people were at home in those units and if one of them had looked out at the right time to see who had run from Martha's place.

I stepped outside and felt my ankle turn again. At this rate I'd be walking down the aisle with a cane.

I looked down at the concrete slab that passed for a patio and saw I'd stepped on the edge of a book. I bent and picked it up without thinking. I grimaced, but the damage was done. My fingerprints were stamped on the red leather cover with or over someone else's, someone besides Martha.

I grabbed my shirttail and held the book in it. Using the material to protect the pages, I riffled through it quickly. It was a diary or a journal, the kind with all blank, lined pages. Its pages were more than half filled with a pretty, straight up and down penmanship. By the dates marking each new entry, I could see Martha wrote in it frequently rather than daily. When I glimpsed the name *MAC,* I knew it was time to call William and grabbed my cell.

I'd just pressed the 9 of 911 when the glass door on the powder-blue unit slid open, and Mrs. Wilson stepped out.

Without a thought, I dropped the journal into my purse. No way did I want her to see it and ask questions about it, maybe even demand I leave it here. It was something for William's eyes only.

I needn't have worried. She didn't see me. Her eyes were red, and she kept sniffing and wiping her nose with a crumpled wad of tissues. She stood staring at the conifers for a few minutes. Then she took a long, shuddering breath.

"Are you all right, Mrs. Wilson?" I asked.

She jumped and turned, her eyes wide and fearful. Her hand came up to cover her heart when she saw it was only me.

"You scared me out of ten years," she gasped. She patted her chest rapidly. Then as fear fled, I could see suspicion replace it.

"What are you doing here? Why are you in Martha's house?" She began to move slowly backward toward her door. "I never saw you here before."

"Sure you did." Maybe she wasn't as sharp as I'd thought. "We talked out front."

She shot me a scathing look. "I know that. Before today. And you shouldn't be here. No one should be here. Martha's dead." It was a wail. Clearly she'd cared for Martha. "I called the police and told them there had been people here. I told them *you* were here."

"Good," I said, holding out my phone. "I was about to do the same thing."

She blinked, uncertain what to think of me. I couldn't blame her.

"How did you learn about Martha?" I asked.

"That phone call? That was my friend Jennie. She heard about it on the TV." Tears filled her eyes and rolled slowly down her wrinkled cheeks. "She was so nice."

"That's what I hear." I smiled sadly. "I wish I had known her."

Mrs. Wilson drew back like I'd slapped her and I knew I'd said the wrong thing.

"If you don't—didn't know her, what are you doing here?" She shook her finger at me. "You go away. Right now."

"I want to wait for the police," I said.

"No. You go. Now." Her voice quavered with distress, but her eyes were determined. She stepped back until she was at her door. She leaned, clearly reaching for something just inside. When she drew her hand out, I stared in disbelief at the object she held. She clutched the burglar bar for her slider and she swung it through the air with all the panache of a knight wielding his broadsword.

"Go," she ordered as the rush of air from her mighty swing brushed my face.

"But—"

"Go!" She took a step toward me, her weapon raised. Clearly her years with Sergeant Major Wilson and the army had rubbed off on her.

Feeling like a Great Dane being chased by a miniature dachshund, I went.

FIVE

Being chased by an amazingly spry eightysomething-year-old lady was very unnerving, especially by one as intent on bashing me as Mrs. Wilson. When I jumped into my car, I half expected her to use her burglar bar on my windshield.

Instead she stood panting on the front walk and I had visions of her keeling over on the spot from a massive coronary; all the blame would be mine.

"But, honestly, officer, she came after me."

"Yeah, right. Hands behind your back." *Snick, snick* clicked the cuffs. "You have the right…"

As I drove away, I watched her in my rearview mirror in case she did collapse. The last I saw of her before a curve in the road hid her from view, she was giving the bar a final shake in my direction.

Now that I was safe, I became very curious about the man who had lived so many years with a woman as feisty as Mrs. Wilson. Had the sergeant major been Special Forces or some such highly trained group? Had he come home from work each day and taught her all he knew? Was their home life the Wilson version of Clouseau and Cato in the original Pink Panther series as they stalked each other from room to room?

I had just taken my seat at my desk back at the newsroom when my phone rang. William to tell me off about Mrs. Wilson and Martha's place?

"Is this Merrileigh Kramer, award-winning journalist?" a man asked, his familiar voice booming down the line. Though he was reticent by temperament, he always projected on the phone like an out-of-work actor auditioning for a last-ditch opportunity at a starring role.

I pulled the phone away from my ear and stared at it in disbelief. Why was Ron Henrey, my former editor back in Pittsburgh, where I had cut my reporting teeth first as an intern, then as a staff reporter, calling me?

"Are you still there, Merry?"

I jammed the phone back against my ear. "I'm here, Mr. Henrey."

"Surprised you speechless, eh?"

"Something like that," I admitted. He was certainly high on my list of People I Never Expect To Hear From.

"Congratulations on winning that Keystone Press Award. We taught you well, I'd say."

"I'd say," I agreed.

There was a little silence while I tried to imagine why Ron Henrey was contacting me. Certainly he wasn't calling to interview a hometown girl made good. That would be an assignment given to a features reporter, the *Chronicle*'s equivalent of someone like me or Edie.

Besides I hadn't made good enough to be worth an article.

"I bet you're wondering why I'm calling," he said.

I made a little agreeing noise, which proved to be all the encouragement he needed.

"We'd like you to come back to the *Chronicle,* Merry. We'd like you to write two or three features a week and have your own column."

Then he named a salary that made me blink in astonishment. I wouldn't exactly be rich, but from my present perspective, I'd be close. The cynic in me, rarely used, kept looking for the catch, but I couldn't see one. Since I'm not a very practiced cynic, it's often hard for me to find the fly trapped in the ointment. However, the rose-colored glasses I wear with practiced ease illuminated a wonderful vista.

My own column! Real money!

I'd been asking Mac for a column for the past several months. He only looked at me and, cynic extraordinaire that he was, said, "In about ten years, Merry. When you finally grow up."

I glanced at Mac, sitting at his editor's desk by the great glass window that looked down from his second-floor perch onto Main Street. He was typing away on his PC, and I felt like a traitor to *The News* with Mr. Henrey trying to lure me away.

Suddenly Mac looked at me. "Hey, Kramer, when you're finished, I need to see you."

As I waved acknowledgement, I tried to imagine Mr. Henrey yelling across the *Chronicle* newsroom at me. Never happen. First off, the room was too big.

Secondly Mr. Henrey, for all his booming phone voice, was a model of propriety. He would either IM me or give me a discreet *bring* on my desk phone.

"What do you think?" Mr. Henrey was still speaking, booming as ever. "Interested?"

I realized I was smiling. I also realized Jolene was watching me smile and would demand to know why as soon as I hung up. No way was I telling her. I might as well stand on my desk and emote like Mr. Henrey because everyone would know before nightfall.

"May I think about this?" I asked. "You've taken me by surprise."

"You have a week," Mr. Henrey yelled genially.

Long enough to develop an acid stomach as I debated the pros and cons, but not long enough to get an ulcer. "Sounds fine."

I hung up, still not believing the offer. Jolene, dressed in a yellow narrow-strapped cami top and a denim miniskirt in spite of the scraped knees, pounced.

"What? Why were you smiling? And don't try and tell me it was Curt whispering sweet nothings in your ear. He doesn't yell in the phone."

Curt! I blinked in disbelief. I'd been so caught up in the unbelievably good offer and so busy being impressed with myself that I hadn't even thought of my fiancé. Granted I'd moved to Amhearst to learn to be independent, to stand on my own two feet, but a girl should at least wonder what the man she plans to marry in less than two weeks would think about moving.

Probably not much. He was as much Amhearst as Jolene and Mac.

There was nothing for it. I'd have to call Mr. Henrey back and decline his offer.

Maybe not, kid, the perverse part of me said. *He's an artist. Artists can paint anywhere, right?*

Hmm, thought the nicer me, jumping much too quickly to agree. *That's true.*

"Come on," Jolene prompted. "Give."

I tried not to look guilty as I scrambled for something to say that wasn't a lie but wasn't exactly the truth, either. I squirmed under her relentless gaze.

She stood and walked across the narrow aisle that separated our desks. I half expected her to stick her index finger under my nose and demand an answer. Instead she spun the little basket of cheery flowers that sat on my desk, checking for dead blooms among the pale yellow double begonia, the miniature pink rose, the crimson geranium and the pale blue dianthus. A regular Gertie the Gardener, Jolene focused the same intensity on her plants as on her insatiable curiosity. As a result the newsroom resembled a nursery with greenery on every available flat surface and a row of the healthiest African violets I'd ever seen lining the sill by Mac's great window.

Suddenly Jolene turned and stuck that index finger with its lethal nail, today a deep crimson, right under my nose. I noticed that her broken middle nail was already repaired. "Talk, Merry. I'm not your best friend for nothing."

Paralyzed, I stared at that nail.

"Kramer," Mac called. "I asked to see you when your call was finished. Remember?"

"Gotta go, Jo. The boss commands." With great relief I rushed to Mac's desk.

"You owe me one," he said as I stood at parade rest before him.

"What?"

"I saw that bit of action." He jerked his head in Jo's direction. "I saved you from a fate worse than death."

"It's not quite that bad."

"Ha! I've known her longer than you have."

"Yeah, yeah. The exclusive Amhearst club."

"You're just jealous because you didn't grow up here."

I thought of Martha Colby who had. "I'm sorry about your friend."

Mac turned grim. "Thanks. Me, too. She was a special girl."

"Did you know she had your name tattooed on her shoulder? In a heart?"

"My name?"

"*MAC*. You can see it clearly in one of the pictures."

He rustled through the printouts of all the pictures I'd taken with Jo's phone until he found the one I was talking about. He touched the tattoo with his forefinger and shook his head. "I didn't know." He looked out his window, his eyes vague.

I waited, feeling somewhat awkward.

Two things happened at once. Mac's phone rang and the back door opened. Curt strode in.

Mac, all business once again, waved toward Curt as he reached for the phone. "Go assure him you're all right while I take this call. Then come back here. I've got a feature assignment for you."

As I went toward Curt, I was sure I was wearing a goofy grin. I still had a hard time believing that this tall, wonderful man loved me. *Really* loved me. At times my past "romance" with Jack came back to haunt me, bringing with it all the doubts it had created. I was learning to take Curt at his word, but sometimes it was hard. Right now it was easy because of the look of concern in his eyes.

When he pulled me into his arms, I melted. I wrapped my arms around his waist and rested my cheek against his chest. *Thank You, Lord,* I thought for the many thousandth time. When I recalled my previous relationship and what I had thought was love, I was appalled at my stupidity. The real thing with Curt made Jack appear a foolish narcissist and me an immature idiot in love with love.

"Are you okay?" Curt asked, his voice gruff with emotion. His cheek rested against my hair.

"I'm fine," I said into the placket of his white knit polo. "Really."

"That's what you always say," he growled. He kissed the top of my head. "As you race into danger."

An old argument. I saw my experiences as my job. He saw them as my disregarding danger and being impulsive. He was doing better at learning to accept the situations reporting sometimes put me in than I was at learning to curb my fools-rush-in-where-angels-fear-to-tread tendencies, such as going in Martha's place.

"No danger this time," I assured him.

"You always say that, too." His arms tightened.

I pulled back and looked up at him. "I'm okay. Really."

"Yeah, yeah. Like finding someone dead is just an everyday occurrence."

A picture of Martha flashed as quickly as a hidden subliminal ad might and I felt tears gather. Curt saw them and leaned down, giving me a brief, hard kiss.

"My tough little reporter," he muttered in my ear.

A very loud throat clearing made me glance at Mac, who was standing pointedly at his desk, looking at us. I also noticed Jolene watching with great interest. At least Edie made believe she was working.

Curt waved at Mac and stepped back. "I can take a hint."

Mac nodded and took his seat.

Curt grabbed my hand and gave it a squeeze. "I'll see you tonight." He grinned and for the first time I noticed the suppressed excitement simmering about him. "I've got the most incredible news!"

"What?" I asked eagerly. "The big commission for a new painting?" I knew a large corporation was talking with him about an original work that would be reproduced as the cover of their annual report. The huge painting itself would hang in their corporate headquarters.

He shook his head. "I'll tell you tonight. But think about how you like North Carolina."

"North Carolina," I said to his departing back, visions of the Outer Banks rising with memories of a camping trip with Mom and Dad and Sam when I was a kid. Or were they in South Carolina? Or both? I never could keep those two states straight. "I thought we were going to the Pacific Northwest for our honeymoon."

SIX

"Are you familiar with Good Hands?" Mac asked me.

"As in the insurance people?" I held my hands together. "You're in good hands with—"

"No, not them. The guys in town who do stuff for people."

I felt a very faint flicker of memory, but nothing I could grab hold of. Can you have senior moments in your late twenties? "Stuff like what?"

"Repair houses for needy people. Fix cars for single moms and widows. Do minor plumbing and home decorating."

"Guys do home decorating?" Now there was an interesting picture—guys hanging pictures and putting up curtains. *No, no, Ben. You know orange doesn't go with purple. Try it with the chartreuse.*

"There are women who do that, I think." Mac thrust a brochure at me. "They're celebrating ten years of doing stuff and I'd like an article about them. Profile the guy who runs the organization, name of Tug Mercer.

Get interviews with some of the people who work with him and quotes from some of the recipients of their help. You know the drill."

I glanced through the brochure and noted Pastor Hal's name as a member of what was called the Board of Overseers. Then that faint flicker burst into a full memory of a few months back when the Good Hands director had given a talk one Sunday morning, a combination testimony and pitch for more workers. I'd liked his enthusiasm for what he clearly saw as a mission from the Lord.

Senior moment survived.

"Sounds great, Mac. I'll get right on it." I turned to leave.

"Wait." Mac shuffled through the stacks of papers on his desk. "Another assignment for you." He pulled out a public relations article, the kind organizations and businesses regularly sent to us, hoping for coverage about some aspect of their activities. Usually the articles didn't provoke much of a response, but every so often one was worth a follow-up. Obviously Mac felt the sheet he held represented one of those.

"They've finally hired Trudy McGilpin's replacement at Grassley, Jordan and McGilpin." He thrust the paper at me. "Guy named Tony Compton. Do an article on him."

Trudy had been a hometown girl who grew up to be Amhearst's mayor as well as a very good attorney. Her death had rocked the town. Taking her place would be a very hard job. Tony Compton better be tough, savvy and able. He needed to be able to live up to the near sainthood status now conferred on Trudy. I half expected that any day I'd receive word that she was about to be beatified, Amhearst style.

As I took the paper on Tony Compton, I saw that Mac had Dawn Trauber's picture taped to the outside of the top drawer of his desk, a good place for it since it would be buried if he tried to set it on his littered desk. She was laughing, her eyes slightly squinted against the sun, her hair blowing in the breeze as she tried to hold it off her face. She looked absolutely lovely. And she was, inside and out.

What would be her reaction when she learned *MAC* was tattooed on the shoulder of a dead ex-girlfriend? I didn't think she had any illusions about Mac, but emotions and intellect often don't march in step. The hearts of smart people who should know better are regularly broken. I know that from experience.

Mac saw me looking at the picture and glanced at it himself. With a sad smile, he reached out and traced her cheek with a finger.

"It'll all work out, Mac," I said earnestly.

He didn't exactly roll his eyes, but he came close. "Thanks, Pollyanna."

"Pollyanna wasn't an idiot, you know. She was just optimistic. I'm optimistic, is all. I'm hopeful."

"She wasn't a real person, Merry. And she was treacly sweet."

"Sure she was real. As real as any other fictional character. I read all her books when I was a kid. My grandmother had them." I smiled at the memory. "I loved them."

He smirked. "I'll bet."

"And what's wrong with being sweet? Or optimistic?"

He glanced back at Dawn's picture. "Dawn's sweet and she's an optimist."

I thought about Dawn and the work she did with girls in trouble. "I agree she's sweet and optimistic, but she's also a realist and a woman of faith."

"Faith is just optimism by a different name," he said.

"Oh, no. Faith is knowing things you can't see and being certain of things you can't touch. And it's believing even when you don't understand."

He shook his head. "That's too vague for me, but if it works for you..." He gave a cynical smile, grabbed a piece of paper and began to write.

I recognized dismissal when I saw it. I returned to my desk and called Tug Mercer, asking for an appointment at his earliest convenience.

"*The News* is going to do an article on Good Hands?" I could hear the pleasure in his voice. "How cool is that! How's ten tomorrow morning?"

Wednesday, 10:00 a.m. I noted it on my calendar.

Before I called Tony Compton, I did a quick computer search on him. There was lots of material on everything from his education (Bucknell University, University of Pennsylvania Law School) and his past employment (Harrison, Ritter, McCorkle and Compton in Harrisburg) to the shockingly sad death of his fiancée, the daughter of state representative Martin Gladstone. Valerie Gladstone had been found stabbed to death three years ago, her body found in her apartment, apparently the victim of an unknown intruder. Congressman Gladstone and Tony Compton had offered a substantial monetary reward for any information leading to the apprehension of the killer, but there were no results.

Immediately my heart bled for this man and his loss, and when I called him, I almost apologized for bothering him. I had to remind myself that three years had passed. Though his pain would never go away, my mentioning it would seem strange so long after the horrible event.

"Wonderful," he said when I told him what I wanted. If his strong, authoritative voice was any indication, he was a man comfortable with himself and life, a man recovered from the depths of his grief. Maybe he could deal with Trudy's legacy. "How about tomorrow? Say, four-thirty?"

After I hung up, I turned to Jo. Before she could nail me about the phone call from Mr. Henrey, which I knew she had not forgotten because she never forgets anything, I said, "So tell me about Ken Mackey."

She made a face and blew a raspberry. Since Jolene tended to look at most people with some degree of contempt, her response didn't surprise me. What surprised me was the obvious depth of her dislike.

"Pretty bad, huh?"

"Worse." Her lips compressed.

When she said nothing more, I held out my hands toward her. "So give."

"They *say* he's reformed." Her skepticism was evident. "But I have my doubts. If there was ever a poster child for recidivism, he's it. I couldn't believe it when I heard he was living with Martha."

"Recidivism?" Was that really the word she wanted?

"Yeah, you know. Sent back to jail or wherever. Back to your old bad ways."

It was the word she wanted, all right. "He's an ex-con?"

She nodded. "He's got a rap sheet as long as my arm. In and out of juvie for years, then a five-year stint for robbery and another for vehicular manslaughter, though to be honest, I don't think he'd have been convicted in that accident if it weren't for his previous problems with the law."

"Good grief!" Why would a woman live with someone like that? No wonder Mrs. Wilson hadn't taken to him. "Was he known to be violent?"

Jo shrugged. "No more than other guys like him. Too many beers and they'll go at it with their fists over some imaginary slur. He went at it once with Reilly back in the old days." She shook her head. "Pitiful."

"Who won?"

She looked at me as if I were nuts. "Reilly, of course.

Of course. The fists comment made me think, though. "Did you ever hear that Ken hit Martha?"

She shook her head, obviously disappointed that she had to admit something positive about him. "He's always had a short fuse and I'm sure his time in jail didn't help that any, but he liked to think of himself as a charmer." She grinned. "I used to call him Charm Boy. He hated it. But he must have been doing better if someone as nice as Martha was willing to live with him."

"Would he take advantage of her, do you think? Let her pay the bills, buy the groceries, stuff like that?"

"Probably. Thick on charm, thin on responsibility and reliability."

Thoughtfully I began a Google search to see what more I could learn about Martha and about Ken Mackey. There was next to nothing about Martha, but I was surprised at the amount of material on Ken. He even had his own blog where he generously shared his views on the problems of the world. Every so often, he said something unexpectedly profound or insightful. Whatever else Ken was, he wasn't stupid.

When the back door of the newsroom opened and William Poole entered, his craggy face set in determined lines, I smiled at him, assuming he wanted to talk to Jolene and me about finding Martha. I hadn't yet stopped to give my statement.

He nodded briskly at us and continued past our desks to stop beside Mac's.

"Uh-oh," Jo muttered.

The tattoo, I thought. *MAC*. That was why William was here. *Oh, Lord, please don't let it be my Mac who killed Martha!*

Mac offered William a seat, something he never did for me or the others on staff. William sank down, his back to the newsroom, and the two began talking quietly, William writing Mac's comments in his notebook.

"It's only because they knew each other," I said to Jolene. "That's all."

"Huh." Grabbing her watering can, she rose and

began moving around the room, watering her thriving jungle. I noted that each plant took her closer to the two men and that the closer she got, the less water the plants demanded. She had just gotten close enough for some really good eavesdropping when William stood abruptly.

"We'll talk again later," he said and strode from the room.

We all watched him go, Jolene with speculation, me with anxiety, and Mac with a frown and a touch of what looked to me like distress or maybe worry. Or fear?

He blinked and became all business. "Jolene, you're drowning that poor philodendron and watering the floor. Since there's nothing to hear anymore, I'd suggest you get back to work. Or go home and bother Reilly."

Totally unintimidated at being caught redhanded, Jolene walked slowly, gracefully, to the shelf where she kept her watering can. She put it away and grabbed a handful of paper towels, returning to the scene of the inundation and mopping the puddle that had formed on the floor.

Mac pushed back his chair, rose and made for the rear door. His posture was rigid, his lips pursed. "See you tomorrow," he muttered.

I watched the door close behind him. "He's upset."

"Wouldn't you be if the police came to interview you?"

"The police have interviewed me lots of times."

"Yeah," Jo agreed, "but your name wasn't tattooed on a murdered woman's shoulder."

SEVEN

By the time I walked from *The News* to Ferretti's to meet Curt for dinner, I had regained most of my tattered self-esteem lost during the chase by Mrs. Wilson, eightysomething terrorist. After all, Mr. Henrey wanted me. And Curt wanted me.

I couldn't wait to tell him about my job offer. He was always so supportive and encouraging, I knew he'd be delighted for me and would find the prospect of starting our marriage in Pittsburgh exciting. New horizons. New possibilities. The Steelers instead of the Eagles. The Pirates instead of the Phillies. The Penguins instead of the Flyers.

The Chronicle instead of *The News*.

And I'd be back in familiar territory again, no longer the outsider trying to find my place among the raised-in-Amhearst crowd. We could buy a house not too far from my parents. Curt could get to know my brother, Sam, a sophomore at Penn State. I could take Curt to my old church and show him off to all the people I'd known most of my life, especially to

Jack, the old boyfriend. Of course, Jack already knew Curt, but still it would be sweet for everyone to realize I had chosen Curt over Jack. I could show Curt all my favorite places and take him to eat in all my favorite restaurants. We could ride the Duquesne Incline and I'd show him the sparkling city by night from the top of Mount Washington. I'd show him the confluence of the Allegheny and Monongahela Rivers as they formed the Ohio. I'd take him to the Carnegie and Andy Warhol museums. And the zoo. I loved the zoo.

When we had kids, they could go to the same schools I attended and I could still work because Curt would be home to watch them. Not that I expected him to be Mr. Mom, but after all, he was going to be there.

He'd already visited home with me several times. Mom and Dad really liked him as a person and as their son-in-law-to-be. We'd gone back two weekends ago and he'd had a great time playing golf Saturday afternoon with Dad and Sam while I was the guest of honor at a wedding shower thrown by all my old friends. Establishing ourselves would be quick and easy; our life would be built on a firm foundation of love, friendships and church. It didn't get much better.

When Curt walked in the door, all tall, gorgeous and wonderful with his black curly hair and broad shoulders, I was feeling very, very good about our future. God was definitely smiling on us.

Curt leaned down and gave me a quick kiss before he slid into the booth across from me. When he reached for my hands, I gladly reached back.

When Astrid appeared to take our order, she looked at me with a mix of commiseration and curiosity. "Merry, you poor thing! I read about Martha Colby in the paper. It must have been so traumatic finding her."

I knew Astrid was fishing—she was always fishing. She saw herself as Amhearst Central—but I liked her anyway because she was so here-I-am-people-take-it-or-leave-it. I, on the other hand, always felt like shouting, "Here I am. Please like me."

"I've had better mornings," I agreed.

"I'll bet." Astrid now oozed sympathy. "Any idea who did it?"

"Not a one."

"Huh." Obviously disappointed, she pulled out her tablet. "What can I get you?"

We both asked for spaghetti with meatballs and parmesan peppercorn dressing on our salads, another sign of our similar outlooks on life. I gave Curt's hand a little squeeze.

"So how come you're serving?" Curt asked the brassy blonde who usually worked as hostess.

Astrid's smile was sour, as far from her usual sunny expression as could be. "Since Annie quit. She's leaving town to go to college and needs extra time to get ready, whatever that means. She gave us two days' notice—two days! What is it with people today?—and we haven't found a new server yet."

I smiled at her. "Well, think of the tips you'll be getting."

"Oh, yeah," she said. "Ferretti's is a hotbed of high rollers." She turned to leave, then stopped in her tracks, staring at a thin woman with dark hair too long for her age and dark circles under her eyes. The woman was sliding into a booth, newspaper in hand. "Well, well, so it's true. She's back in town."

The woman looked up, saw Astrid staring at her and gave a tight smile.

"What's she doing here tonight?" Astrid frowned. "You'd think she'd be too cut up to go anywhere."

I looked at the woman as she laid the menu aside, began to unfold her paper, a copy of today's *The News*, then paused to pull a pair of glasses from her purse. "Who is she?"

Astrid leaned on our table with both hands and dished. "Esther Colby. Or used to be Colby. I don't know what her name is now. She disappeared a long time ago, thirty years or something like that. Quite a scandal when she walked out on her family."

Astrid shook her head as if she didn't understand such behavior. "I always felt sorry for Steve Colby, who's a nice guy, if you ask me. Left him with their little girl. Of course, he eventually married Nanette, and they have kids, too. But I don't think he ever heard from Esther after she took off." Astrid glanced surreptitiously at Esther. "And now that little girl is dead. Esther should just leave again and let Steve and Nanette grieve in peace."

"Esther Colby?" I watched in fascinated horror as the woman began reading the paper. "As in Martha's mother?"

"Yeah. Quite a homecoming present, huh?"

The dark-haired woman gave a sudden cry. She was

staring at the front page of the paper and I knew exactly what she was reading because I had written it.

Her hand went to her mouth as her face became a mask of horrified disbelief. "Oh, no!"

Astrid paled. So, I'm sure, did I.

"She didn't know," Astrid said. "Now I feel terrible dissing her like that."

I nodded as I watched Esther Colby grab her purse and bolt for the door, the paper fluttering to the floor forgotten. Of course the police hadn't notified her. They probably didn't even know she was in Amhearst. Maybe Steve Colby didn't, either, or, if he did, didn't know where to reach her.

Astrid shook her head. "I guess your daughter is still your daughter, even if you did abandon her." Looking thoughtful, she wandered off toward the kitchen.

I stared at Curt, trying to imagine what it was like to find out your daughter had been murdered by reading about it in the paper.

Curt was watching me, concern evident in his eyes. "Are you okay?"

I nodded. "I just feel bad for her."

He shrugged. "I feel worse for Steve Colby though. And Nanette. Astrid's right. They are nice people."

"How do you know them?"

"Steve was my high school math teacher, believe it or not. Then when I taught, he became a professional friend. Since I stopped teaching, we haven't seen much of each other, but I've been thinking of him all day."

"Did you know Martha?" He hadn't mentioned knowing her earlier today when he stopped at work.

He nodded. "Not well, though. She ran with a different crowd than I did."

"With Mac and his friends."

He nodded. "All of them nice enough in their own way, but too wild for me, especially back then." He grinned. "I was a good kid."

I had to laugh. "I bet."

Astrid showed with our iced teas, salads and crusty Italian bread. When she left, Curt asked, "Is there anything new on the murder?"

I blinked as every horrible memory rushed back like high tide streaming into the Bay of Fundy. I poked at my salad without much appetite.

"Not much new, but I did learn that there was a new boyfriend." I told him all Mrs. Wilson had said, then proceeded to make her wielding of the burglar bar into a lighthearted story. Curt laughed in all the right places and telling the story replaced the image of Martha with that of a little old lady with too-black hair, restoring my appetite.

"Good grief!" I said as I finished. "I forgot. I can't believe I forgot."

I dropped my salad fork on my plate and reached into my purse. I pulled out the diary I'd trod on, taking care to hold it by one corner with my napkin. I showed it to Curt. "Martha's, I think. I found it on the back patio just before Mrs. Wilson came after me."

"How'd it get there?" He reached for it.

I pulled it back. "Uh-uh. Fingerprints. I think either

Ken or the new boyfriend dropped it when they left by the back door. Photos were missing from in the house, too, and the bathroom had been ransacked."

Curt looked at me thoughtfully and I squirmed under his gaze. I braced myself.

"I don't think I'll ask how you know all this, though I'm willing to bet William didn't tell you."

Relief swept through me. He wasn't going to give me a hard time about my B and E.

He continued, "It sounds like somebody covering tracks."

"I think so, too." I frowned as I stared at the red book. "I leafed through it quickly when I found it and I saw the name *Mac*. That scares me, Curt."

Curt looked thoughtful. "You said Martha was hit with a rock, right?"

I nodded, the vision of the blood and hair on the murder weapon making me shudder.

"I can't see Carnuccio doing something like that. He certainly hasn't always been a model citizen, but there's a great distance between womanizing and drinking too much and committing murder."

I nodded. "I agree. And I don't think he'd be seeing Martha at the same time he was seeing Dawn. He's too crazy about Dawn to do anything to jeopardize their relationship." *I hope, I hope, I hope.*

"Yeah, but he is used to women who will sleep with him—and Dawn won't."

Our spaghetti arrived and saved me from having to defend Mac. We spent the next few minutes eating and it was a relief to put the mystery aside. As I twirled my last few strands of spaghetti, I couldn't keep my good news to myself any longer.

"You'll never guess who called me today." I knew I must be wearing a silly smile.

Curt paused with a forkful of meatball halfway to his mouth. He gave me the look that said, "You're right. I can't guess."

"Mr. Henrey!" I gestured excitedly as I said it, forgetting the twirled spaghetti on my fork. The tail end lashed out and a great blob of red sauce flew unerringly through the air to land on Curt's white polo right over his heart. We both started at the red mark, me appalled, he with resignation.

"I almost wore red," he said. "But I told myself that I was mature enough to eat spaghetti without getting it all over myself. I forgot about you."

He looked so forlorn that my guilt meter went zinging over the top. At the same time I had to slap my hand over my mouth to curb my inappropriate laughter. "I'm sorry!"

"I can tell." His voice was sardonic.

"I am. Really. I'll wash it for you. I can get the stain out." I think.

He nodded. "You do realize that this wouldn't have happened if you cut your spaghetti instead of twirling." He pulled one side of his shirt out of his pants.

"I've worried about our union of twirler and cutter. Such a vast chasm of difference. What will it do to our children? And what are you doing?" By now his shirt was completely untucked.

"You can't wash it with me in it." He spoke with a perfectly straight face.

"No shirt, no food," I reminded him and ate the offending forkful.

He gestured to his spaghetti, what little remained, all hacked into tiny pieces. "I've already got the food. What are they going to do? Take it back? And who's Mr. Henrey?" he asked as he tucked himself back in.

I grinned at him. I loved this man. "My old boss at *The Chronicle.*"

Curt raised an eyebrow.

I took a deep breath and said with pride, "He offered me a job, a great job." I gave him all the facts. "Isn't that fabulous?" I leaned back as Astrid cleared our table. "We can buy a house with lots of windows and great light for your studio and it can be near my parents. We can go to my old church. You can paint western Pennsylvania things and have your work hung in western Pennsylvania galleries. And when I get an unexpected assignment, you can watch the kids for me because you'll be home working. Can you imagine anything better?"

I looked at him expectantly and realized with surprise that he had pulled back, literally, leaning against the back of the seat, and figuratively, folding his arms over his chest.

"First," he said, his chin raised in challenge, "if I'm working, I will not be able to watch kids, either in Amhearst or Pittsburgh or anywhere else. You need to understand that. When I'm working, I'm as unavailable as you are when you're working."

"Okay." Inconvenient but understandable.

"I mean it, Merry. I may work at home, but that doesn't mean I'm on call. I'm not."

"I get it." My voice was a bit tart.

"Good." He added cream to the coffee Astrid had just brought. "And when does this marvelous opportunity of yours start?" His voice was still cool.

"As soon as."

"Huh."

That was it? Huh?

"I know it's a surprise," I said, leaning forward, trying to understand his attitude like a good fiancée. "I was surprised, too."

"You didn't contact him first?"

I blinked at the chill washing across the table. "You mean as in apply for the job? Are you kidding? Without consulting you?"

Curt just stared, his eyes sober behind his lenses.

I was offended. "Do you really think I'd do something like that behind your back? We're getting married. Married people make decisions together."

The frost thawed somewhat as he nodded, apparently satisfied that I wasn't as nefarious as he'd feared.

"Give me some credit," I muttered, peeved that he even thought I might do such a thing. And he'd squelched my joy. I felt flat where I'd expected to feel as if I were soaring. I swallowed my resentment, forced a smile and asked, "So, want to move to Pittsburgh with me?" Sensing the wintery atmosphere once again lowering to frostbite temps, I added, "Of course, we would have to give Mac plenty of time to replace me and you plenty of time to get used to the idea."

Curt grunted.

"Should I take that as a yes, I'd love to move to Pittsburgh?"

"Did you already take the job?"

"Sheesh, Curt." I propped my elbows on the table and rested my chin in my palms. "I already told you I wanted to talk it over with you." Where had this stubborn, unreasonable Curt come from?

He grunted again. "I'm not certain this conversation qualifies as talking it over."

"Yeah, well, it would if you'd talk."

Suddenly he leaned over the table, getting in my face. "Do you realize you haven't asked my opinion?"

I drew back and stared at him. "I just asked if you wanted to move."

"That is not asking my opinion. What if I think such a move isn't in our best interest?"

Much as I hated to admit it—and I wouldn't out loud, at least not right now; I was too steamed and too hurt—he had a point. "So what's your opinion? Why wouldn't this be in our best interest?"

"What about my career?" he asked. "Do I just give it up?"

"Of course not." Talk about foolish. "I just said you could paint western Pennsylvania scenes. I mean, you can paint anywhere."

He just stared at me.

"Well, you can. There's sunlight in Pittsburgh and art supply stores and art galleries and anything else you might need."

"And my work with Intimations?" he asked, referring to the gallery in Philadelphia with a branch here in Amhearst.

"They can still show your work. They show the work of lots of artists who don't live locally."

"But I teach for them."

"I'm sure you can teach in Pittsburgh."

"You've checked into it for me, have you?"

"Well, no, but we're not talking the end of the earth here. There have to be lots of people who want to learn to paint there."

He grunted again. "What if I want to keep teaching my students here? What if I want to teach in North Carolina?"

"North Carolina?" Where had that come from? Then I remembered he'd mentioned North Carolina when he'd stopped at the office this morning to see how I was after discovering Martha.

"In the Appalachians." His eyes looked fondly into middle distance.

"You want to teach in North Carolina?" I all but screeched, albeit quietly. Screeching is more tone than volume, more intent than decibels. "But that's too far to commute."

He focused on me, his eyes shuttered to hide his emotions. "I was thinking of something more permanent."

"What?" Surely I didn't understand him correctly. "You want to move to North Carolina?"

"Maybe. You're not the only one who gets job offers, you know."

I was appalled. "Someone in North Carolina offered you a job? But you're self-employed."

He pushed his empty coffee cup aside and leaned toward me. This time he was eager, not displeased. "I got a call this morning from West Carolina Art Institute. They want me to come talk with them about joining their faculty."

"Why you? How you?" North Carolina?

"Apparently one of the art profs was in Philadelphia and visited Intimations. He was impressed enough with my work to look up my Web site. He noted that I taught school before I started painting full-time and that I taught art classes now. Long story short, they approached me about filling a position unexpectedly vacated."

"But what about the academic credentials to teach at a university?"

He looked much too pleased with himself as he said, "I have my master's and with my credentials as a producing, selling artist, they feel it's enough for an adjunct professor."

I frowned at him. "So just like that you want to move to North Carolina? Without talking it over with me?"

"I don't know if I want to move to North Carolina or not. I have to go visit, look the place over and talk with people." He looked at me. "I'd like you to come with me when I go."

"Oh." The man was really serious about this possibility! "I can't. I've committed all my vacation time for our honeymoon." Not that I wanted to go even if I had the time.

He smiled. "I went on the web and checked, and there's a wonderful paper in the area, sweetheart, just the thing for you. You're very fortunate because newspapers are everywhere."

"Right." I stood, feeling betrayed, which I knew was foolish. But he was supposed to be delighted for me, not offering an alternate plan. "But they don't all need another reporter."

He stood to leave, too, and I followed him out. The temperature outside had moderated from the heat and humidity of the afternoon and the soft, long twilight of summer wrapped around us as we walked together to our separate cars, both parked in *The News* lot.

As I hit the electronic key to open my driver's door, Curt swung his arm around my shoulders and drew me close. He kissed the top of my head, then my lips. I wrapped my arms around his middle and kissed him back.

"Don't worry, sweetheart," he said. "We'll figure it out."

"Yeah," I said as I rested my head on his chest. But I didn't know how without one of us feeling cheated. Resentful. There was a good start for a marriage. I blinked back tears as I leaned into him.

Oh, Lord, it's not supposed to be like this! Then I added, *Please change his mind!*

EIGHT

I walked into the Amhearst police station at about eight-thirty Wednesday morning and asked for Sergeant Poole. My stomach was a mass of knots and I had a throbbing headache from lack of sleep. In my purse I carried the equivalent of a ticking time bomb.

That's what I got for reading someone's private diary.

But how could I not?

I stood in the small entry hall beside the Coke machine. The dispatcher looked at me from behind his wall of bulletproof glass and in a metallic voice that emanated from a speaker over my head told me he'd see if the sergeant was available.

I hadn't even finished reading the second wanted poster tacked to the bulletin board near the station's front door when William appeared. He looked especially solemn as he led me into the bowels of the building where the offices were.

"How are you this morning, Merry?" he asked when we were seated in his office.

I smiled wanly. "I'm well," I managed. "How are you?"

I'd worn a V-neck T-shirt and a linen big shirt, both a lovely rose shade that made my cheeks look nice and pink, on the theory that the bright color would give me courage. It wasn't working. I just don't do well with guilt, mine or a friend's. I jumped on a subject that would put off the topic of my visit a few more minutes.

"Did you know that Martha Colby's mother is in Amhearst after thirty or so years?" I thought of the stricken face I'd seen last night at Ferretti's.

He nodded. "She came barreling in here yesterday evening, demanding to know what had happened to her baby."

"Her baby?" This from a woman who had stayed away for so many years?

"Yep." William's mouth curled cynically for a moment, then eased into its normal line. "I do think she was very distressed in spite of the strange situation."

"Why did she come back? Did she say?" I eyed him. "I'm sure you asked."

"I did, but you know I can't talk about an open case with you, Merry."

"Yes, but isn't it strange that she's here when the murder happened? I mean, after not being here all those years?"

He held up a hand in a halt gesture. "Don't jump to conclusions. Just because she's in town doesn't mean she's automatically connected with the crime."

"Well, I think the timing is a bit suspicious."

He shrugged and leaned back in his chair. "Just another little mystery to go with the one you might be able to help me with."

"Yeah?" I sat up straighter, immediately off balance. William usually told me to step back, not give him help.

"Yesterday when Officer Schumann went to Martha Colby's home, she met a very irate neighbor."

Mrs. Wilson. Oh, boy.

"This neighbor, a remarkably agile, clear-minded woman of eighty-three years, told Officer Schumann about a 'housebreaker' whose name she couldn't quite remember, but she thought it might be Joy. She said that the woman was, and I quote, 'a bad un.'"

Housebreaker? A bad un? I almost wished I had my own burglar bar. Then I could challenge Mrs. Wilson to a duel for the slur to my character and she and I could have crossed bars as cavaliers used to cross rapiers.

"Have you any idea who this woman might be?" William looked at me, his craggy face stern.

I swallowed. "Is this woman in trouble?"

"It depends on whether she broke any laws."

I thought of how I'd wandered through all the rooms. "Like what?"

"Did she break and enter? Steal anything?"

I thought of the diary burning a huge hole in my purse. "I'm certain she didn't break and enter. She knocked on the door and it flew open." Okay, *flew* might be an exaggeration, but it was definitely not closed. "She called hello and when no one answered, she went in to be certain everything was okay." Just a good neighbor doing a good deed. That was me. It just happened I did this good deed in the house of a recently murdered woman.

"And what did she find?" William asked, his eyes

watching me like the cat that had cornered the poor little innocent mouse housebreaker.

"She found a pretty house that had already been searched."

"How did she know that?"

"Mrs. Wilson told me—her. Ken Mackey had been there and the new boyfriend whose name she doesn't know. Have you found Ken Mackey yet?" I asked in the hopes I could distract him from my iniquitous behavior.

"No. What else did she see?"

Well, I hadn't really thought that ploy would work. William was too sharp. "She said pictures had been displaced and some things knocked over. She thought some pictures might have been taken. Oh, and the bathroom was a mess."

William suddenly leaned forward and I fought the urge to lean back. "Now my big question," he said, his intense gaze drilling into me. How did bad guys ever keep from spilling their guts when someone like William went after them? Any minute now I'd confess to everything from assassinating Abraham Lincoln to stealing the atomic bomb secrets for the Rosenbergs. "Did she take anything?"

I shook my head so hard I felt like a bobble-head doll. "No! She didn't take anything! And she didn't touch anything, either." I shifted, nervous. My purse shifted with me and I realized I'd just lied to William. "I mean, she didn't intend to take anything. It just sort of happened."

William said nothing, just stretched out his hand.

I reached into my purse and extracted the diary sealed in a plastic bag. It looked so innocuous, so ordinary. How could something so commonplace be so damning?

"I found it on the back patio, sort of like someone had dropped it," I said. "I picked it up without thinking. When Mrs. Wilson came out, I dropped it in my purse because for some reason I can't explain, I didn't want her to see it."

He pointed his index finger at me, his hand in the form of a revolver. "Did you read it, Merry?"

I flushed. "Yes."

He closed his eyes and sighed. The unspoken words, *save me from amateur detectives and newspaper reporters,* hung in the air between us like the dialogue bubble in an old comic. He opened the plastic bag and let the diary fall onto his desk.

Don't open it! Please don't open it. Ever.

Foolish, foolish wish. William picked up a pen and with the retracted end lifted the cover. Holding the cover open with the pen, he used the eraser end of a yellow Ticonderoga pencil to flip through the book page by page, scanning, tucking each page under the pen as he moved through.

Perched there on my uncomfortable plastic chair, my knees together, my hands clenched, I felt like Quisling, that Norwegian traitor in World War II who helped the Nazis. His name was now a synonym for turncoat. Of course, William was hardly the Nazis and turning in a piece of critical evidence wasn't anything like turning on your countrymen. Still, no matter how right and lawful my actions, I knew that in the future *Merrileigh* would be a synonym for a false, fair-weather friend.

I sat as still as I could. Then I saw William's eyebrows rise and he stopped turning and read.

I suddenly felt twitchy all over. I knew exactly what he was reading. Last night as I sat with the diary in bed, leaning comfortably on my pillows with Whiskers purring at my side, I'd sat straight up and yelled, "No!"

Whiskers jumped and snarled at me for wakening and dislodging him. Tail high, he stalked to the foot of the bed where he turned in a circle several times before collapsing with a loud *umph!* I reread the entry dated April 20, but it said the same terrible thing it had the first time through.

Once again, Mac to the rescue. Tall, dark, good-looking—and such fun! Goodbye, Ken. Hello, happiness. How does a girl get so lucky yet again?

Following that were two and a half months of glowing entries about Mac mixed every so often with mention of his temper, the bruises on her upper arms, the broken crockery, ending with a recounting of a visit to the dentist a week ago to have a broken tooth repaired.

I told him I walked into a door, but I could tell he didn't believe me. I told Mac that if he ever touched me like that again, I was going to the police. I mean, he actually punched me in the mouth! As usual he made apologies all over the place, brought me flowers and told me how wonderful I was. No wonder he can convince people so well. Words are his stock in trade.

I'm not sure about anything anymore except that I love him and he scares me. What a mess!

By the time I was finished, I was on my knees beside the toilet losing what little was left of my spaghetti dinner. I sat huddled on the floor leaning against the tub, my mouth tasting sour.

So Mac had come into her life again. That didn't mean he had killed her. It didn't. But what about Dawn? Would he kill Martha to keep Dawn from knowing about her? About his temper? His abuse?

And how did I know it was my Mac Martha was referring to? Surely there were other people in and around Amhearst called Mac. I just didn't happen to know them.

I spent a long time wrestling with myself about turning the diary over to William. Even if it wasn't our Mac, it would put him in a bad position because of his previous relationship with Martha. *Once again, Mac to the rescue.*

But there was really no choice, and so here I sat watching William read the damaging words.

After a few minutes of silence William looked at me. "Who else has read this?"

"No one." I felt sort of offended that he'd even think I'd share something so vital to the case with others.

"Not Curt?"

I shook my head. Of course, if we'd already been married and he'd been there in the middle of the night, I'd have shared it. I also would have cried on his shoulder.

"Jolene?"

"Good night, no."

"Mac?"

Again I shook my head. I had wanted to. I wanted to point to the April 20 passage and say, "Where were you that night? Tell me this isn't you. Prove to me this isn't you."

Of course I couldn't show him or ask him about it. That was William's job. If Mac was involved somehow in Martha's murder, he had to be held accountable.

Oh, Lord, please! Not my Mac.

William looked at me sternly as he tapped the diary with the Ticonderoga eraser. "You can't mention this to Mac, Merry."

"I know."

"And you can't write about this."

I looked at him, utterly miserable. "I have to write something. What can you give me?"

"The investigation is moving—"

"Yeah, yeah, I know. Apace. That is absolutely no help."

He grinned, his shar-pei wrinkles shifting like a crumpled sheet of paper suddenly smoothed. "You could help us locate Ken Mackey."

"Is he a suspect?" Maybe he could take the heat away from Mac.

"We just want to talk with him given his friendship with the victim."

"I'm sure Mrs. Wilson told Officer Schumann that Ken has moved out."

"But not where he went."

"She didn't like him," I said. "He was dirty and smelly."

William nodded. "He races motocross. I'm sure he's often both."

I thought of the pictures of him that littered the Web. In each he was muddier than the last or he was tumbling head over heels into a fence or another rider. There had to be safer, cleaner ways to have fun, but dirty and smelly it certainly was.

"Mrs. Wilson likes the new boyfriend," I said. "Mac." Mac, who had taken Ken's place, if not in the house itself, certainly in Martha's heart. "I bet Ken resented Mac a bunch."

"Maybe." William let the diary fall shut. "But we have to locate him to find out."

NINE

Before I left home to meet with Sergeant Poole, I'd sent Mac several inches of story about Martha, the investigation, the murder weapon and Mrs. Wilson minus the burglar bar. Now I sat in my car and, using my wireless laptop, added a couple of lines about the police seeking Ken Mackey to talk with and sent it to Mac, too. He would cut as needed to fit today's edition.

As a result I was able to go straight from the police station to my interview with Tug Mercer of Good Hands after one quick stop at a Turkey Hill Minit Mart to grab a Diet Coke and a cream-filled Tastykake coffee cake.

Tug was a big blond man, not so much tall as large. His navy polo shirt with the stitched Good Hands logo stretched over his shoulders and body, but he wasn't lumpy or chubby. Just solid. Impressive. When he shook my hand and gave me his open smile, I automatically smiled back.

"I'm more surprised than anyone at what Good Hands has become." He sat behind his desk with me facing him in a sturdy molded plastic chair. His office was in an old house that belonged to one of the churches in town and had been converted into cheap office space for various Christian enterprises. The office walls held pictures of before and after houses, doubtless Good Hands projects, as well as several framed prints that showed collections of hand tools or plumbing equipment or architectural paraphernalia. A manly office appropriate for one who oversaw the repair of dilapidated homes.

"How long has Good Hands existed?" I asked

"The idea first came to me twelve years ago," Tug said, "but it took two years to figure out exactly what it was that God wanted me to do and the best way to do it."

I looked up from my trusty notepad. "Explain."

Tug leaned back in his chair. "I was sitting in church minding my own business when I got the idea of helping needy people in substandard housing in Chester County. It was one of those God-thoughts that is so outlandish that you automatically doubt it. One proof that the idea is from God is if it doesn't go away but continues to eat at you. This idea eventually ate me whole."

He grinned happily at the memory of being consumed with his God-thought. I liked Tug and his enthusiasm for what he considered his call from God. I could easily see him with a tool belt around his waist and a hammer in his hand. I wondered if Mac realized how much of a faith story this article was going to become.

I checked the tape recorder on Tug's desk just to be certain the wheels were still turning. They were. "What did you do before you got the idea for Good Hands?"

"I taught school. I loved it and the kids. Often in the summers I took students to help out in Appalachia through the Appalachia Service Project. We helped repair houses, fixing and painting and building all kinds of things. So when the idea for Good Hands first came to me, I knew what would be involved. Trouble was, I didn't want to leave my teaching."

A knock on the door drew both Tug and me.

"Sorry, Tug, but we just wanted to say hi and goodbye before we go home." A pretty, petite woman with huge brown eyes and brown hair pulled back in a ponytail stood in the door. "I forgot you had a meeting."

Tug jumped to his feet. "Come on in, Candy. Meet Merry Kramer from *The News*. Merry, my wife, Candy."

"Hi, Merry." Candy Mercer gave me a brilliant smile as she held out her hand. After we shook, she met Tug at the corner of his desk. He leaned down and gave her a kiss on the cheek. She reached up and patted him gently.

Behind Candy slouched a girl I judged to be about fifteen or sixteen, much fairer than her mother, several inches taller and many pounds heavier. Her daddy's little girl, at least physically. She would have been pretty except for the sullen look and the heavy black makeup rimming her eyes. She wore a baggy black T-shirt and a black pair of sweatpants in spite of the warmth of the day. Her round cheeks were pale and her brown eyes sad.

"And this is Bailey," Tug said. He smiled at Bailey as he gave her cheek a kiss, too. "We're trying to decide if she's turning goth on us and hasn't gotten all the way there yet or if she just has a thing for black." There was no rancor or mockery in his voice.

"Dad," Bailey muttered, embarrassed, but she half smiled. Clearly this topic was a family joke.

"I certainly hope you never touch that beautiful blond hair with black dye," I said fervently. "I've rarely seen such a wonderful color. Or colors." I peeked behind Bailey to see how far down her back the yellow, gold and silver strands fell. It cascaded over her black backpack and I couldn't help but grin at the incongruous sight of a couple of knitting needles sticking out of the backpack and through her hair. Lovely, fuzzy, pale yellow yarn pushed against the heel of one. How fascinating that the semigoth was working with such a delicate shade, one that would be absolutely wonderful with that gorgeous hair, especially if she eased up a bit on the black eyes.

Bailey flushed at my compliment, with pleasure, not embarrassment, I thought. Her parents looked at her with love and worry.

"Can you sit on it?" I asked, remembering that not too long ago my hair had been long like that, though not that stunning shade. Cutting it had been part of my decision to remake my life, as had been my move to Amhearst.

She shook her head, pushing one side of the glorious sweep behind an ear. "I keep it cut at my waist. It's hard enough to get it dry now. I don't need any more."

"It's absolutely gorgeous. You're very lucky. And guys do seem drawn to blondes, you know." I grinned at her.

She dropped her eyes and shook her head, her pallor returning.

Touchy topic. I wondered how hard it was for her with her excess weight, how much the kids teased her at school, how much she disliked herself. Being her age could be so hard!

"I've been telling Merry how Good Hands got started," Tug announced in the small silence that followed Bailey's apparent embarrassment.

Candy followed his lead and pointed a finger at him. "Did you tell her how I started wondering if all you were ever going to do was plan this organization and its purposes and never get around to actually fixing up houses?"

Tug took her out-thrust hand. "I'm sure you'll tell that part better than me."

Candy smiled at him as he continued to hold her hand. She turned to me. "Tug's got two friends who are in the business world, and they met with him for breakfasts, lunches, dinners, evening snacks—you name it. They planned Good Hands meticulously, applied for and got not-for-profit status, wrote mission statements, vision statements, anything you can imagine. Not that all that wasn't good. It got Good Hands off to a wonderfully sound start, but I thought they'd never get beyond planning."

"That's because we didn't know how to get local needy home owners to want our services. We just couldn't walk up to someone and say, 'Your house needs fixing. Let us do it for you.' Also, there's no way to know by looking whether the house was owned by the people living there or rented. We aren't in business to do what landlords should be doing."

I saw Bailey sort of flinch. She grabbed Candy's arm. "Come on, Mom. I need to get home."

Candy nodded. "Tell Merry about Simon," she ordered as she leaned forward to kiss Tug goodbye.

"Wait a minute," he said though he leaned in for the kiss. "Before you go, show Merry your storeroom."

"Storerooms, plural," Candy corrected. "Come on, Merry." She turned and walked down the hall. I followed her while Bailey stayed with Tug. Candy opened one room stuffed with used furniture.

"All donated," she said proudly. "We'll refinish it or reupholster it as needed."

She opened a second door and I saw a room lined with shelves, all but one stacked with fabric in various bright prints. Three sewing machines sat in the middle of the room.

"Sheets, blankets and quilts, mostly," Candy said, waving at the shelves. "We go to Appalachia two or three times a year and buy quantities at wonderful prices at the various mills located down there. We use the sheets to make great curtains and bed hangings."

"What's stored there?" I pointed to boxes stacked on the other shelf.

"Wallpaper borders."

As we walked back to Tug's office she described how she and a group of women with skills in interior design would go into a house that Good Hands was working on and redecorate if asked.

"We always put a rocking chair in a baby's room,"

she said. "And we try to make the master bedroom as beautiful as possible, especially for the single moms who for financial reasons have to put themselves last. Freshly painted walls, a colorful border and new sheets with curtains that match can make such a difference to a woman."

My head was swimming with the scope of all Good Hands did as we reentered Tug's office. Candy collected Bailey, who was sitting in an unhappy lump on my chair, pausing at the door to again remind Tug to tell me about Simon, the mailman.

"Yes, dear." He made himself sound put-upon, but it was obvious that the bond between Tug and Candy was deep and lively. Just like Curt and me, I thought—until I remembered North Carolina.

Lord, please change his mind. Help him see how perfect going home will be.

I watched as Tug walked Candy and Bailey to the office door, then stood there, his eyes sad as he watched them down the hall and outside.

"I worry about her," he said. "She's so unhappy."

Bailey of the glorious fall of soft gold, Bailey who was very overweight and wore the ugliest clothes she could find, Bailey of the excess eye makeup, Bailey who wanted to be different but wasn't rebellious enough to become fully goth.

"It's the age," I offered. "She'll probably slim down and wash away the black gunk in a year or two."

"From your lips to God's ears. It's just her older sister was so easy! Candy and I were spoiled." He walked back to his desk and sat down. "Now let me tell you about our friend Simon, the mailman, who had the poorest mail route in Amhearst and found us our first clients. He told us which people we could trust to have legitimate needs and he told them that they could trust us not to rip them off."

By the time I returned to *The News,* I had more than enough information about Good Hands for an article, but I wanted more. I wanted that magic three points of view. Tug had given me names so that I could contact some of the nearly one thousand volunteers who gave up their Saturdays to help the many home owners—mostly widows, seniors and single moms—who were somehow scraping by but with no extra funds to hire someone to repair things and no time or knowledge to make the repairs themselves. I also wanted to interview some of the people Good Hands had helped and find out about the difference the assistance had made in their lives.

"At first all we thought about were the houses," Tug had said. "Then we started to notice the people and the serious problems they often faced. Our motto became Hope, Joy, Dignity, reflecting what we hoped to offer our clients.

"Then we finally realized that often our clients had spiritual needs, too, so we've now incorporated spiritual goals into the program. We ask each client to have a ten-minute Bible study with us when we come. One or two of each team have volunteered to help this way and the clients seem to like being cared for and prayed for in this format."

I was feeling really good about the world and the

way some people made positive differences until I walked through the door of *The News* and saw Mac, Jolene and Edie standing around my desk. Larry, the sports guy, was frowning at me from his desk across the room.

I froze, every instinct telling me to turn and run. "What?"

"Pittsburgh, Merry?" Jolene said.

"*The Chronicle,* Merry?" Mac said.

Edie just looked at me with disappointment like an aura about her.

I blinked. "How in the world?" I hadn't told anybody but Curt and I knew he wouldn't talk about my job offer, especially with the topic so tender and unresoloved between us.

"If you're going to argue about something with Curt, don't do it in public," Jolene said, pointing one of her lethal nails at me. "Astrid is the town crier."

In that moment, Pittsburgh's siren call sang incredibly sweetly. A large city where no one knew my name. A large city where Curt and I could slug it out in one of the shops in the Strip and people would barely blink. Here in Amhearst I might as well be living in a glass house.

I sniffed, sat down and activated my computer. "Mac, go edit something and leave me alone. Jo, go water your plants. They look dry. Edie, go write about some great Chester County house or some wonderful, quirky Chester County resident. If and when there's anything any of you need to know, I'll tell you."

I began typing furiously. Not that anything I was

writing made sense. I might as well have been typing *the quick red fox jumped over the lazy brown dog.*

The phone rang and I answered to find Tug Mercer on the line.

"I've contacted several of the people that Good Hands helped and they're looking forward to talking to you. In fact, if you're free tomorrow afternoon, Bailey can go with you to introduce you."

No wonder Good Hands had accomplished so much if Tug was always this on top of things. "Tomorrow sounds fine. One-thirty?"

When I hung up, I found I had also calmed down. I looked surreptitiously at my three coworkers, all carefully ignoring me. When Curt and I moved to Pittsburgh, I'd miss them. A lot. They had become good friends. No, they had become more, woven into the everyday fabric of my life in a way that made me feel cared for and appreciated, the threads of our lives woof and weft one to the other. Yes, I would miss them even if I wouldn't miss Astrid.

I sighed. *Lord, let's get this over with quickly, okay? Pittsburgh, okay?*

TEN

I left the newsroom just after 4:20 to walk to the old building down the street from *The News* for my interview with Tony Compton. As I exited, I smiled sweetly at everyone and said not a word. Jolene and Edie smiled sweetly back, something that was unnerving coming from the acerbic Jo. Mac just glowered.

They cared that I would probably be moving. I walked with a spring in my step; I really was going to miss them. I was.

I smelled the fumes in the old building before I noticed the clean look of the newly painted hallways. The building had always been clean and well kept, but brown walls a shade just this side of mud had made it depressing. Now it welcomed me.

Halfway up the inner stairs to the offices of Grassley, Jordan and McGilpin, I met Mr. Weldon, the custodian, coming down, a ladder taller than he in his hands.

He stopped and smiled at me. "Merry! What a wonderful delight."

I grinned at him. Mr. Weldon played in the bell choir

at church with me and he loved it just as I did. I should say he played a bell. He and his wife shared high C and D.

"I don't trust myself to play two," he always said. "Too hard what with flats and sharps and all. But one I can manage. And Mother wants me to be happy and play, so she takes the other." And the Weldons would smile at each other. I got a kick out of their eccentricity and delight out of their affection for each other.

Mrs. Weldon always reminded me of Barbara Bush, aging without self-consciousness, taking the wrinkles and gray hair as just a part of life. Mr. Weldon was a plump man of indeterminate years with graying hair that curled no matter how short he cut it.

"I'd shave it all off," he told me one night after bell practice, "but Mother likes to run her fingers through it." He sighed, then grinned. "Ain't life tough?"

I'd laughed all the way home.

Now I said, "The place looks very nice, Mr. Weldon. The bright beige makes the hallways look light and welcoming."

He looked at the freshly painted stairwell with some anxiety. "You really like it? I'm afraid it's going to show every bit of dirt and every fingerprint. That wonderful brown didn't show anything."

"You might have more dirt to tackle, Mr. Weldon, but the light color's much better for a dark old building. Take my word for it."

He bobbed his head at me. "I got carried away by this wonderful paint sale, Merry, and then after I bought it, I had to use it. No returns." He sighed. "I can never pass up a good sale. That's why Mother never lets me have any of the credit cards and only a few dollars at a time. I'm what they call a shopaholic."

I had to laugh at the image of Mr. Weldon elbowing his way to a sale table.

"And never let me loose in the Home Depot or Lowe's," he continued. "I love those stores. I had so much fun buying the paint for the new lawyer's office—he didn't want the soft lavender that Ms. McGilpin had, surprise, surprise—and then I couldn't resist the lure of the sale and got the beige, too."

"Well, it was a good purchase."

He eyed the walls again, then grinned happily. "Bright." And he continued downstairs with his ladder as I continued up. At the landing I turned right toward the door that now read Grassley, Jordan and Compton, Attorneys at Law.

I pulled the door open and walked into the reception area.

"Yes?" asked a young thing who was actually wearing a skirt. Required professional attire? Maybe I ought to do an article on business dress in this era of casual business clothes. I hadn't worn a skirt to work in years.

"I have an appointment with Mr. Compton. I'm Merry Kramer of *The News.*"

She consulted her appointment book. "Of course, Ms. Kramer. Mr. Compton is due back from court at any minute. Won't you take a seat?" She indicated a comfortable arrangement of deep stuffed chairs grouped around a coffee table covered with magazines.

I took a seat, stuffing the decorator pillow behind my back. A tall man had picked these chairs, never thinking about a shorter person whose legs weren't long enough to sit back in the chair. Then again, maybe that was why the decorator pillows were here. I checked the magazines, impressed not only with the selection but the current dates. I decided to take advantage of the enforced downtime and read without guilt. I was halfway through the second magazine when the door to the hall opened and a tall, dark-haired man in a navy pinstriped suit and crisp white shirt walked in.

"Hello, Annie, my angel," he said with a charming smile. "How's it going?"

"Fine, Mr. Compton, sir." The receptionist fairly glowed at his attention.

"I hope no emergencies have cropped up while I've been gone." He paused by her desk and she turned bright red with pleasure.

"No emergencies, Mr. Compton."

He nodded and smiled full wattage as he loosened his power tie and unbuttoned the top button of his shirt. "Good. I'll be in my office," he said. "No calls, please." He started toward a closed door where the opaque glass still read *Trudy McGilpin.* He stopped and frowned. "When is that man going to change the name?"

His voice was mild, but he was clearly annoyed.

Annie swallowed like it was her fault the door hadn't been renamed. "He changed the main door." She pointed.

"So he did. Well, that's a step in the right direction." He grabbed the knob of the door to his office and opened it.

As Annie's eyes swiveled from the door back to the lawyer, she spotted me, forgotten under the spell of her boss. "Uh, Mr. Compton, your four-thirty appointment is here."

He stopped, spun and saw me for the first time. He gave me the same charming smile he'd bestowed on Annie. I could see why Valerie Gladstone, his late fiancée, had fallen for him. If receptionists and strangers got this wattage, imagine what someone he cared for got.

Annie stood quickly and said, "This is Merry Kramer from *The News*. Remember?"

"Of course, of course." He walked to me, his hand extended.

I stood quickly, knowing he didn't remember at all.

"Ms. Kramer, forgive me for keeping you waiting. It's a pleasure to meet you." His two-handed grip swallowed my hand. "Please, let's go into my office."

"Mr. Weldon just finished painting it for you," Annie said helpfully. "It's a beautiful color."

Tony Compton nodded and stood aside to let me precede him. When it was obvious that Compton's attention was on me, Annie sat with a sigh. Poor kid. Unrequited love was a very hurtful thing.

The walls of the office were a beautiful color, a rich crimson that sat well with the crisp white window frames, crown molding, baseboards and bookshelves. On the floor under boxes of unpacked papers and books lay a cream oriental rug patterned in crimson, fawn and black. Behind the massive cherry desk was an executive's chair covered in crimson leather. Assuming Tony

Compton had asked for the walls to be crimson, he had either a great decorator or an unusually strong sense of design and color for a guy.

"Wow," I said, looking around. "Very lovely."

"I was going more for you-can-trust-this-guy than lovely," he said with a smile. I couldn't help but notice that when he smiled, the corners of his dark eyes crinkled like those of an old-time cowboy too long in the sun. Interesting on a man whose job kept him indoors most of the day.

He indicated I should sit in one of the two visitors' chairs placed before his desk. They reminded me of the two upholstered chairs my mother had sitting at either end of her dining room table, except these were crimson leather instead of blue on blue brocade.

As I sat down, I told myself that the paint fumes weren't bothering me, weren't making my nose twitch.

"So, Mr. Compton," I said, "what made you decide you wanted to practice law in Amhearst?"

"Please, call me Tony." His smile was so charming I found myself smiling back automatically. He must beguile juries easily with that charisma, especially the women.

"So, Tony, what made you decide to practice law here in Amhearst?"

"As you probably know—and I'm assuming someone as professional as you did your homework—I practiced for several years in a large firm in Harrisburg."

I wondered how he knew how professional I was, but I had to admit it was a good line. I found myself sitting straighter.

"I liked being in a firm at the center of state politics.

There was always something exciting going on. But after a while the furious pace and the constant stress began to wear on me." He aimed the high-wattage smile at me again.

I nodded as if I understood and wondered whether a smile that came so easily and so frequently meant much. I also told my stomach that the stronger-than-usual paint vapors were not making me feel ill. After all, throwing up in a man's freshly painted office is hardly professional.

Tony stood abruptly, for once sober-faced. "I don't know about you, but these fumes are getting to me. If I didn't know better, I'd think that man used oil-based paint, the smell is so strong."

Gratefully I stood, too.

He walked around his desk and put his hand on the small of my back to guide me toward the door as if I didn't know where it was. He smiled down at me, one of those smiles that says you're-the-most-fascinating-woman-I've-ever-seen-and-I'm-so-glad-you're-here-my-day-would-have-been-a-total-loss-without-this-time-with-you.

Quite frankly not many people had ever smiled at me like that. Just Curt and once in a blue moon, Jack, the old boyfriend. And maybe the kid I had a crush on my freshman year in high school. I loved it when Curt looked at me with such genuine love and delight. Jack and the kid from high school no longer counted. With Tony, even though I knew it was part of his schtick, I felt flattered.

Women of Amhearst, look out!

Maybe I should wave my engagement ring in his face, let him know I wasn't on the market, but I wasn't sure it would deter him. Based on my limited sampling—Annie and me—I'd say that women automatically brought out his charm. I wondered what Mac would say if I wrote that Tony Compton was a ladies' man. Hire him at your peril.

He turned me gently toward the door. "Let's just walk down to Ferretti's and have a bite to eat while we finish this interview. I never did get any lunch."

I stepped out quickly just to prove I could get to the door all on my own and felt my left foot catch on the edge of one of the boxes waiting to be unpacked. I put out a hand to stop my fall. It slapped against the office wall right by the door and for a few seconds I balanced precariously over the box that had tripped me. Tony solved my problem by shoving the box out of the way with one foot while he grabbed my free wrist and hauled me upright.

"Are you all right, Merry?" He managed to sound as if he actually cared.

Safe on my feet, I stared at the smudgy hand print I'd made on Tony's freshly painted wall, then at my red hand. "I am so sorry!"

He smiled again, but it wasn't the easy smile of earlier. This one seemed a bit forced. "Not to worry. The paint guy—"

"Mr. Weldon," I said.

"What?"

"The paint guy."

"Ah. Well, he can fix it, I'm sure. Now we'd better get you cleaned up."

He led me out to the reception area by a new grip about my other wrist, my red hand suspended in front of him as if he feared I might accidentally touch something. Maybe his blindingly white oxford shirt? Annie stared at us openmouthed.

"There's the washroom." Tony pointed, releasing me.

I went into the room and shut the door behind me. I pumped soap from the pretty dispenser on the sink and lathered up. The first sign that I had a problem was when the lather didn't turn red. I rinsed my hands, and my palm was as red as ever. I made a face at myself in the mirror. Definitely oil-based paint. I had a new understanding of why Mrs. Weldon didn't let Mr. Weldon have any credit cards. Any man who was a soft enough touch to buy oil-based paint for walls just because the price was good was a dangerous man if unsupervised.

Well, he could give me some turpentine to remove the paint and I'd be fine. I stood in the front hall and called his name, my voice echoing most satisfactorily up the stairwell. No answer. Tony banged on the locked door of his office though we both knew it was useless. Mr. Weldon had gone for the day and was probably home having dinner with Mother.

I sighed as I slid into a booth at Ferretti's across from Tony. What I needed was Curt and his artist's supply of turpentine. I smiled to myself. What I needed was Curt, period. Then I frowned. In Pittsburgh.

Astrid appeared and held out menus to us. She looked at me curiously. Then she spotted my red palm as I reached for the menu.

"Hah! Caught redhanded!" She looked from me to Tony and laughed at her sad joke.

"Astrid, this is Tony Compton, the new partner in Grassley and Jordan."

"Yeah, I know," she said. "He's in here a lot."

Tony smiled that gorgeous smile, this time focused on Astrid. "We're already old friends, aren't we, Astrid?"

She twinkled back at him. Astrid. Twinkled. The words had never before gone together. I shook my head at the power of Tony's charm.

When Astrid left with our order, I reached into my purse for my notebook and tiny recorder. "Let me ask you a few questions while we wait."

Tony leaned forward, all his attention concentrated on me.

Please, Lord, I thought, *don't let me twinkle.*

"Okay," I said, trying to be as professional as I could manage in spite of my red hand and Astrid's stare over the computer monitor where she punched in our order. "Why did you decide to leave a large practice like the one where you were a partner in Harrisburg and come to a small town like Amhearst?"

"Because small towns are full of fascinating people like you."

Give me a break! "And Harrisburg didn't have any fascinating people? I'm sure the governor would be upset to know your opinion of him."

He grinned. "I decided I wanted to be in a place with a slower pace of living, a place where I would know people and they would know me, a place where people would recognize the name Tony Compton as someone interested in helping them."

I wrote quickly, wanting to get the quote accurate in case the recorder's sound was bad. Suddenly Tony reached out and grabbed my left hand. I was so surprised I dropped what I was holding.

He turned my hand palm down and looked at my engagement ring. He ran his thumb over the stone. "Very nice."

"Thank you."

"Someone is a very lucky man."

"Thank you."

"Local guy?"

I nodded. "Curt Carlyle."

"The artist?"

I nodded, feeling self-conscious as he continued to hold my hand. I tried to pull free, but he held tighter.

"There was one of his paintings on the wall of my office when I came. Some stone building somewhere."

"Curt's paintings are worth many thousands of dollars, you know." Okay, so I overstated a bit, but his offhand disregard for Curt's work made me mad. And the big, complicated paintings were worth between $2,000 and $5,000.

Tony smiled, not the least put off by my show of pique. "Getting married soon?"

"A week from Saturday."

He looked up from the ring and concentrated all his charm on me again. "Then I still have time."

Oh, pul-ease! "Tony, don't." I was feeling more and more awkward by the moment, especially when Astrid arrived with our salads, saw our hands and slapped the plates on the table with a sniff.

"Thanks, Astrid," Tony said without taking his eyes from me.

I looked up apologetically and she looked at me with a raised eyebrow. "Redhanded," she muttered and stalked away.

Red-faced, as well, I thought as I felt myself flush. I pulled harder and Tony finally released my hand with another smile, not, I'm sure, because I wanted him to but because he wanted to eat and needed both hands. No lunch.

I concentrated on pouring the little plastic container of blue cheese dressing on my spring greens, tomatoes and cucumber slices. By the time I was halfway through the salad, I'd convinced myself that Tony had meant nothing by holding on longer than was polite. I was just being supersensitive. I listened to his stories of life in Harrisburg with interest. He was a great raconteur.

I had taken my last bite of salad and laid my fork down when Tony suddenly reached across the table and took my hand again, this time my right one. He turned it palm up. He traced the life line crease across the red flesh.

"Tony," I remonstrated, tugging.

"Do you have turpentine at home?" he asked, ignoring the tug and my tone of voice. "If not, I'll get you some."

"I don't have any, but Curt will have some."

He looked at me, his face for once serious. "I hope he deserves you."

I decided I liked him serious more than smiling. At least I felt the emotion was sincere. "What would you do," I asked slowly, "if your fiancée had a great job opportunity in, say, Pittsburgh? Would you move there for her?"

"Hypotehtically speaking?" he asked.

"Oh, of course," I assured him.

"If you were the fiancée, I'd move in a minute. Hypothetically speaking. There are plenty of excellent law firms in the greater Pittsburgh area and one would certainly be happy to have someone with my experience as part of their firm."

"Huh," I said, loquacious as always. Why hadn't that been Curt's answer?

A shadow fell over the table and I looked up to see Curt standing there.

"Well, hi," I said. "This is a surprise." Immediately I tried to pull my hand free, but Tony just tightened his grip again. Unless I wanted to look like we were arm wrestling, I was stuck. I fired Tony a fierce look, but he was busy smiling at Curt.

"Don't let me interrupt," Curt said, staring at my imprisoned hand with a raised brow.

"Oh, you're not," Tony said with a smile, this one very cool. "Merry and I were just enjoying dinner together, weren't we, sweetheart?"

ELEVEN

Sweetheart? Get real. "You're not interrupting anything," I assured Curt. "I'm just interviewing Tony for the paper. He's the new partner at Grassley, Jordan."

"Mmm," said Curt, clearly unimpressed.

I gave one more mighty yank in an attempt to reclaim my hand and Tony released me. My arm flew back and I cracked my elbow on the edge of the back of the bench seat, sending lightning bolts surging up to my shoulder.

"Yow!" I grabbed my arm and rubbed.

Both men ignored me in my hour of pain. They were too busy eyeing each other like a couple of male dogs wanting the same fire hydrant. I frowned. *Bad analogy, Merry, at least the part about the fire hydrant.*

Tony held out his hand. "Tony Compton. Merry and I were just enjoying each other's company, right, darling?"

I rolled my eyes. Now I was darling? Tony was clearly an agitator.

"I'm Curt Carlyle. Merry's fiancé." He gave Tony's hand the barest of shakes.

When Curt's hand was free, I grabbed it. He didn't seem to notice, so I squeezed as hard as I could.

Curt broke away from the stare down with Tony and deigned to look my way. "I stopped at the paper, but you had already left," he sort-of accused, though I knew his ire wasn't really directed at me but Tony.

"I had this appointment with Tony. I thought you had a meeting." That didn't sound like while-the-cat's-away-the-mouse-will-play, did it? Because I definitely wasn't interested in playing.

"It was canceled. I thought we could have dinner together." He looked at my empty salad plate.

Astrid took that moment to appear. "Hey, Curt. Welcome." She smiled widely at him and he smiled back. I couldn't remember an evening of so many smiles.

Astrid placed a steaming plate of eggplant parmigiana in front of Tony with great care. She plopped my fettuccine Alfredo down with a thud, grabbed my salad dish and stalked away.

"Well, I'm in the doghouse." I glanced at Curt. "She's on your team."

He smiled. "She's a very nice lady."

And I was certain her version of this dinner à trois would be all over town by tomorrow.

He took a step back. "I'll let you continue with your interview."

I was reluctant to see him go. I found that these days I was always reluctant. I couldn't wait until we were married and there'd be no more good-nights of the leaving kind. I was very open to good-nights of other kinds, though.

"Nice meeting you, Carl," Tony said cheerfully.

"Um." Curt inclined his head. Then very deliberately he bent and kissed me hard on the mouth. I kissed him right back.

He paused a few inches from my face and said softly, "By the way, I got the call today that I got the commission for the painting that will be the cover art on next year's Fetteroff Allied Services annual report. A very nice chunk of change."

"Sweet!" I was delighted for him. "I'm proud of you." I gave him a congratulatory kiss.

Tony cleared his throat and looked at his watch. "I don't mean to be intrusive here, but I have a meeting this evening. We need to finish our business."

I had my doubts about both his lack of desire to be intrusive and the meeting, but Tony was right about one thing. This was supposed to be a business dinner, at least as far as I was concerned. I smiled apologetically at Curt.

He'd already taken several steps toward the front door when I called, "Do you have any spare turpentine?" I held up my red hand.

He shook his head in disbelief, but his smile was warm.

A half hour later Tony and I left the restaurant.

"Where's your car?" he asked as we walked down Main Street.

"In *The News* lot."

"Let me walk you there."

"You don't have to do that." *I wish you wouldn't do that.* I was finding Tony didn't wear well.

He insisted, so I gave in. It wasn't worth a discussion. When we arrived at the car, he grabbed my red hand again, tuning it palm up and looking at it.

"Poor palm."

"It's only paint," I said. It wasn't like I was going to lose the hand or anything.

He acted like I hadn't spoken. He lifted my hand and kissed the center of my palm. I think he meant it to be dashing and romantic, but it tickled and I had to stifle a giggle.

It was a relief to climb in the car and drive away.

When I got back to my carriage house apartment, I was surprised to see Curt waiting for me in the parking area. He climbed out of his car as I climbed out of mine.

"Hey!" I was delighted to see him. "I didn't expect you."

He held up a plastic container. "Turps." He took my hand and studied it. "How'd it happen?"

I told him about tripping over Tony's box. "Poor Mr. Weldon. He's going to have to fix my mistake."

"And he'll be happy to do it. You know him. Now let's go clean you up."

We walked to my front door past the lilac tree that had been so terrifying to me last winter and was now full and green. I missed the wonderful froth of blooms that had crowded it a couple of months ago. The air had smelled so sweet every time I walked past, and I cut great bouquets for my dining room table and my desk at work.

Whiskers met us at the door. I didn't even have

time to put my purse down before he began butting me in the ankles.

"Are you out of food, baby?" I asked as I rubbed my hand down his back. "We'll fix that problem right away."

Whiskers seemed to understand and led the way to the kitchen. Once there, he sat by his empty dish and stared at me. I grabbed his dry food and poured some into his bowl. He sat, still staring.

"Sorry, baby. No canned food tonight. You had plenty this morning." I turned to Curt. "Let's get me cleaned up."

We moved to the kitchen sink and he opened the container he'd brought. The strong smell of the solvent made me want to sneeze. He took my hand and held it over the sink in a firm but gentle grip.

"I can do this on my own, you know," I said.

He grinned lazily at me. "But I want to do it for you."

My heart went pitter-pat. Yowzah, I loved this man.

Slowly he drizzled turpentine over my palm, then began to rub with his thumb. The fluid instantly turned red. More turps. Dish detergent. Rinse. More turps, his thumb working the creases in my palm and fingers. I closed my eyes and leaned against his shoulder, enjoying his TLC. No wonder people paid big bucks for a good massage.

When my hand was once more its normal self, we went into the living room and sat on the sofa. Curt leaned against the arm and I leaned on him. Whiskers immediately jumped up and nestled close. Apparently I was forgiven for not coming through with wet food.

We talked in a desultory manner, Curt telling me the details about his new commission, me telling him about Good Hands, Tug, Candy and Bailey.

"I was thinking that it would be a wonderful thing to give each of the people Good Hands helps a Curt Carlyle print," I said. I glanced up to see his reaction.

"Those prints sell for a hundred dollars each, sweetheart," he said. "I can't just give them away in quantity and at the same time ask others to pay full rate."

"Yeah, but you make up a small version for promotion and stuff. What about them?"

"They're not the high quality of the big prints."

"But if you signed them and they were matted, I think people would be proud to have one."

He nodded. "Maybe. Let me think about it." Then he looked at me sharply. "You didn't volunteer me, did you?"

I sat up straight. "Hey, I've got some smarts. I'd never do that without asking."

"Easy, sweetheart." He kissed my forehead. "Just asking. I didn't mean to offend you."

Mollified, I settled back against him. We sat quietly, the only noise Whiskers's purring. Curt started playing with my hair, his fingers killing the mousse effect. Soon I'd be a flathead. Well, he might as well get used to it. I looked a lot worse in the morning. I relaxed and enjoyed.

"I got a call from the art institute today," he said.

So much for relaxation. "Um?" I thought I sounded noncommittal and neutral.

"They want to interview me next week."

I sat up and turned to face him. "And you're going?"

"Of course."

I thought I detected a wariness underneath. What did he think I'd do, throw a tantrum at the very idea? Well, I might have felt like it, but I had too much class. Besides, I was too busy trying to figure out how to show him that Pittsburgh was much better for us than North Carolina.

Where was Jolene when I needed her? She was great at stuff like getting her way.

"This is so last minute, the tickets'll cost the school a fortune." Which meant they really must want him, I thought without pleasure.

He shrugged. "That's their problem. I'm just glad we don't have to pay for them."

We don't have to pay? Consciously or unconsciously he'd hit on just the right word. We. He wouldn't accept the job in North Carolina if I didn't want him to because we were a *we.* So what was the harm in visiting? Let him see the place and get it out of his system.

I took a deep breath. "Okay, go and check the place out." I hoped he was impressed with my magnanimous spirit. "But don't make any commitments, okay?"

Curt nodded. "I wouldn't without your input and agreement."

I nodded and tried to push my niggling fear to the back of my mind. It wouldn't stay there, so I voiced it. "What if we never reach an agreement?"

He was quiet for a minute, thinking it over. "I could always say I'm the head of the family and you have to do as I say."

"Now that'd really make me feel loved."

"Mmm. Whatever happened to 'Where you go I will go, and where you stay I will stay. Your people will be my people and your God my God'?"

Dirty pool, pulling out scripture, but I wasn't thrown. I had a good answer which just proves there's a lot to be gained from listening in church. "That quote from the book of Ruth is a daughter-in-law talking to her mother-in-law. It's not a wife to her husband even if lots of people do use it at their weddings."

He looked at me with my smug smile. "You're too smart for my own good."

"And don't you forget it, bucko." I kissed him. "Now, when you get home from North Carolina, we'll make a list of good and bad for both places."

He sighed and stared at the ceiling for a few seconds. He didn't like lists nearly as much as I did.

"All right," he finally said. "We'll make a list." He turned his dark gaze to me. "But don't think that just because I love you, I'm going to cave and agree to move west. This opportunity may be too good for me to pass up."

I looked at him and knew he meant what he said. There was no way I was going to cajole him into doing what I wanted just because it was what I wanted. Even Jolene lessons wouldn't be of any help here.

Oh, Lord, You're going to have to break him for me.

TWELVE

When I got up on Thursday morning, I pulled on white slacks and a navy blouse with a sailor collar that was piped in white. I couldn't remember the last time I'd seen anyone over five wear a sailor collar, but I liked it, so who cared? It made me feel jaunty, like a yachtsman standing before the great chrome wheel, my feet planted wide on a teak deck.

While I ate a little tub of strawberry-banana yogurt and crunched a piece of my Jewish rye washed down with Diet Coke, I planned my day. First, visit the police station to seek the latest on Martha. Then begin work on the Tony Compton piece and set up a time to get a picture of him in his new office. Have lunch with Jolene and Edie. Visit Good Hands clients with Bailey. Take my off-season clothes over to Curt's and figure out where they could be stored.

Here I grinned. Moving my things slowly into his home made the wedding, which could seem a mirage despite all the preparation being made, take on a vivid realness. There was something very intimate about my blouses and his shirts hanging side by side, my towels and his sitting together in the linen closet.

Then I'd cook dinner for Curt and go to bell choir practice.

All in all, an interesting day.

I scraped a can of food into Whiskers's bowl as he wrapped himself happily around my ankles. Trying to trick him, I mixed some of his dried food with the wet. He began to eat and I heard the *tap, tap* of dry nuggets as he spat them on the floor. He'd snack on them during the day, but he didn't like them interfering with his enjoyment of the wet food.

Intelligent pets can be trying.

When I left the apartment, I met Mrs. Anderson, my next-door neighbor for the past three months, on the little porch we shared. An elderly lady who was to her generation what Jolene was to hers, Mrs. Anderson had an extremely active social life. I rarely saw her, but when I did, she was always dressed to the nines for some meeting or luncheon or dinner. Upon occasion I had seen her and other of her blue-haired friends at Ferretti's.

Not that Mrs. Anderson had blue hair. No, sir. Her hair was suspiciously golden-brown with patches of a strange purple at her temples that I finally figured out came from her rouge, which she brushed on with a little too much enthusiasm. She wore bright, youthful colors and while she didn't trot along at the same clip as Mrs. Wilson, she was pretty spry. She was a friendly, alert, intelligent woman. I wanted to be like her when I grew up.

Which is why I was so startled to see her in her

bathrobe with her hair uncombed and her face devoid of makeup.

"Did you hear him, Merry?" she whispered. "Or see him?"

"Who, Mrs. Anderson?" I looked around for an interloper.

"That man last night." She peered over my shoulder as if she expected to see him standing behind me. "He was skulking around the house."

Our carriage house held four apartments, two down and two up. An extremely quiet teacher, who was currently in France for the summer, lived above Mrs. Anderson. A pimply faced, very young couple whose ambition was to be roadies for a rock group used to live above me. Last month they'd gotten their wish and were on the road with a local band called Don't Rush Me. No new tenants had taken their place, assuming they had broken their lease.

That left Mrs. Anderson and me, and I would be gone in another week.

"What was this man you saw doing?" I asked, fighting the urge to look over my shoulder, too.

"I don't know." She hugged herself and rubbed her hands up and down her upper arms. "I was having one of my sleepless nights—I have about two a week—and I was sitting in the rocker by my bedroom window that looks out on the alley when I saw him. He was dressed in black and slinking along." She pursed her lips. "Anyone slinking along at three in the morning is up to no good."

I had to agree with that thought. "Did you call the police?"

She shook her head. "All I saw was a man in black. I didn't see him do anything. I don't think they come for everyone who sneaks down alleys. He'd have to commit a crime for them to be interested."

I nodded. "Maybe it was just a husband stealing home and he didn't want his neighbors or his wife knowing he'd been out so late, especially if he'd been with another woman or something."

Mrs. Anderson relaxed visibly. "See? It could be something that innocent, couldn't it? Though if Mr. Anderson ever tried to sneak in like that, I'd have had a word or two for him, let me tell you." She sniffed. "Innocent, my foot."

I grinned. I was willing to bet that Mr. Anderson had had no more chance of stealing in late than Sergeant Major Wilson.

"I'll just keep my ear out for any reports of trouble and if I hear something, then I'll call the police. I wrote it all down—the times and all—so I wouldn't forget."

"He didn't see you, did he?" I don't know why, but the thought that he might have made me nervous. Finding dead people tended to activate any latent tendencies toward anxiety.

"No, no. I was sitting in the dark. A glass of warm water and a good rock and I'm usually back to sleep. If I turn on the lights, I'm awake for the rest of the night." She reached for her door. "Well, I won't keep you any longer, dear. I feel much better for having talked with you. Have a good day."

With a wave, I headed for the parking area located on my side of the building. I pulled out my keys and hit the button to unlock the driver's door. I loved the little electronic gadget. It was so cool to open the car when you weren't even near it yet.

I slid behind the wheel and slipped the key in the ignition. The engine turned over without protest. I was about to slip the car into Reverse when Mrs. Anderson appeared on the walk, waving her arm frantically at me.

Uh-oh. I undid my seat belt and slid out, leaving the motor running in my hurry.

"What's wrong?" I called as I jogged toward her.

"I forgot to tell you," she began, holding out a piece of paper.

What she was going to tell me was lost in the roar of a great explosion very close by. The force of it sent air waves rushing at Mrs. Anderson and me, and we were both thrown through the air. I ended up in the lilac bush, the branches poking at me even as the leaves cushioned my fall.

I clawed my way out of the lilac, slashing my left palm on a freshly pruned length of old growth. Mrs. Anderson! She was a little old lady. Fragile bones and all that. What did this fall do to her?

And what had exploded?

I staggered away from the tree and saw Mrs. Anderson sitting on the ground looking dazed, holding her right arm.

"Are you all right?" I asked as I dropped down beside her.

"I'm fine, dear. Just knocked my arm."

That's when I noticed that I was dripping blood on

my white slacks. My new white slacks, slated for the honeymoon.

"Oh dear," Mrs. Anderson said. "Your hand!"

I stared at the blood welling in my palm. The landlord who wouldn't even give us higher-wattage lightbulbs in the parking area and the front walk had had the lilac pruned, leaving sharp, jagged branches for a person to fall on?

"I'm fine," I said, knowing the cut wasn't serious.

She looked beyond me. "I'm afraid your car isn't."

I turned and caught my breath. My wonderful little car was blazing and it hit me that if it hadn't been for Mrs. Anderson, it would have been my funeral pyre.

I began to shake.

THIRTEEN

William and his people arrived in a dead heat with Curt, whom I called as soon as I hung up from 911. We all stood around the dead carcass of my vehicle and stared at it as it smoked and made groaning noises as it settled and the metal contracted. I was pressed hard against Curt's side, my injured hand wrapped in a kitchen towel and held up in the air so it was higher than my heart.

"It'll lessen the bleeding," Mrs. Anderson assured me.

With my good hand I held Mrs. Anderson's hand, in which she clasped the piece of paper she'd waved at me, consequently saving my life. She held her other arm to her chest, her wrist already swelling.

"Mrs. Anderson needs to go to the hospital to have her wrist checked out," I said.

"An ambulance is on its way," William said.

Mrs. Anderson straightened her shoulders. "I do not need an ambulance, young man."

He grinned, his face undergoing that fascinating

seismic shift. "I'm sure you don't, ma'am, but please let the EMTs tell you whether you need a physician to look at your injury, okay?"

Mrs. Anderson seemed mollified, if only barely, and we turned our attention back to my car.

"What could have happened?" I asked. "I never heard of a car just blowing up like that."

"I'd guess it was intentional, sweetheart," Curt said, looking pale and strained. "Right, William? She's right that cars don't just explode."

One look at William confirmed that he agreed with Curt's analysis and that he didn't like the fact one little bit.

Come to think of it, neither did I.

"Do you think it has something to do with that dead girl you found?" Mrs. Anderson asked. "Maybe you saw something that would incriminate someone." She had rallied amazingly well from her short flight in the air, her injured arm aside. But then it wasn't her car that had fried.

"I didn't see anything!" I exclaimed.

"Maybe you did and just don't realize it," she persisted.

There was a small silence as we all thought about that.

Then I shook my head emphatically. "I saw nothing."

"Then why?" she asked.

No one had an answer, so we just stood and watched the car smolder while we waited for the EMTs.

When they arrived, they checked out Mrs. Anderson, who insisted she was fine.

"But you have a broken wrist," one of the EMTs told her. "You need to get it set."

"So set it," she told him.

He bit back a smile. "We don't set bones, I'm afraid."

"You can save my life, but you can't set my bones?"

"I'm afraid that's right," he said.

"Ridiculous," she muttered. "But I'm not riding in any ambulance. I am not sick."

Another EMT examined my cut palm. "It'd be a good idea for you to get stitched up," she said. "Only take a few minutes in emergency."

I didn't want to ride in an ambulance any more that Mrs. Anderson did. I looked at the unhappy woman and the equally unhappy EMT trying to talk her into climbing aboard the ambulance.

"How about we take Mrs. Anderson to the hospital with us when I go for my stitches?" I suggested.

This happy solution let the EMTs leave and let us watch when the bomb squad from the state police arrived in answer to William's call. They circled the car, but they couldn't do much of anything until the smoking metal skeleton cooled. They talked briefly among themselves, then offered their consensus that there were two possible scenarios. One was a timed device activated when the engine turned over.

"Thirty seconds, max, from when I turned the key until the explosion," I said. "Why the delay?"

Everyone shrugged.

The other option was that the bomb was activated by my cell phone, which I carried in my purse like most other women.

"Like in Iraq?" Curt said. "IEDs?"

"What?" Mrs. Anderson and I looked at him without understanding.

"Improvised Explosive Devices. You call a cell phone near the device and the ring detonates it."

"Did you hear your phone ring?" William asked me.

I shook my head. "But then I had gotten out of the car." A chill ran through me. "How could he know that I had gotten in the car? He'd have to have been watching, wouldn't he?" Talk about eerie, weird, strange, odd, uncanny, bizarre. I took a deep breath. When I started with the list of synonyms, it was time to take a firmer grip on my emotions.

William nodded. "He saw you get in but not out. He could have moved someplace for cover and placed the call."

"He must have planted the device during the night," Natalie Schumann said.

"He did." Mrs. Anderson held out her paper. It had taken her some time to find it after the blast had blown it out of her hand. She'd finally discovered it in the garden of the house two doors down.

Now she offered it to William. "I saw him for the first time last night at—" she peered at the paper "—2:54 a.m. He was sneaking down the alley toward the parking area, though I didn't realize then where he was going. He was carrying a black bag."

She turned to me. "That's what I wanted to tell you when I yoo-hooed you after you got in your car. He carried something the first time I saw him, when he went *to* the parking area. The second time I saw him—" she peered at the paper William held "—was 3:14. And the bag was empty. He had it crunched in his hand." She crunched a make-believe bag in her hand. "So he wasn't a husband trying to slip home like we thought, because he went down and then back. That's the other thing I wanted to tell you, Merry."

So many questions and no answers swirled through my mind as we waited in the emergency room for treatment with Curt as our Good Samaritan and chauffeur. Mrs. Anderson's X-ray confirmed she had a broken wrist bone. While they set and casted her, I got shot in the hand to numb the palm and then got stitched up after they painted the area thoroughly with bright orange disinfectant.

"Will this stuff wear off soon?" I asked, thinking of the wedding.

The doctor shrugged and we left, Mrs. Anderson wearing a handsome sling over her housecoat.

"Did you see Millie Long in there?" she asked as we walked across the parking lot. Her voice was full of distress.

I shook my head. "I don't know Millie Long."

"She came in an ambulance because they thought she had a heart attack."

"Oh, I'm so sorry. Is she a good friend?"

"Sure, but that's not the point. She saw me looking like this!" She looked down at her bathrobe and slippers. Her good hand went to her head. "And my hair!" She groaned. "I can't stand it!"

"I'm sure she understands," I said, though if she came in with a possible heart attack, I doubted that she even noticed Mrs. Anderson, let alone her appearance.

Mrs. Anderson sighed. "You're too young and beautiful to understand. At my age a woman must be vigilant if she wishes to preserve her image."

"Sounds like Jolene sixty years from now, doesn't it?" Curt asked and I had to laugh. Then a thought struck me.

"Curt! If it was the murderer who planted the bomb—and I don't know who else it would be—what if he tries to do something to Jo, too? She was with me when I found Martha."

"Then he must have a personal death wish," he said, his voice dry.

"I'm serious! Is Jo in danger? We have to warn her. We have to talk to William."

I borrowed Curt's cell and called Jo. Mrs. Anderson listened avidly.

"Reilly," Jo yelled without moving the phone and I thought my ear would pop. "You've got to save me!"

When I could hear again, I called William. "Thank you, Merry," he said. "The thought has occurred to us, too. I would suggest that you not go anywhere alone until we know what's going on. In fact, why don't you just move in with Curt?"

"Can't. It wouldn't be right."

"Oh, come on, Merry. Everyone lives together these days. And everyone knows you're getting married, so it's not like you're shacking up."

"Can't, William. He and I are both committed to premarital chastity, just like the Bible says."

"Well, just live there if you don't want to sleep with him."

I looked at Curt's strong profile as he drove us

homeward. "We're chaste, William. Not dead." I hung up to his laughter.

After we helped Mrs. Anderson into her apartment and got her settled with a nice pot of tea, we went to my place and I called Mr. Hamish, owner of a local car dealership that also handled rentals. In the months I'd lived in Amhearst, he and I had become good friends.

"What happened this time?" he asked eagerly as soon as I identified myself. He had rented me cars on numerous occasions and he thought I lived a very interesting life.

"A car bomb."

"Wow!" he said with awe. "How fascinating."

"That depends on whether or not it's your car," I reminded him.

Curt, who drove me to Mr. Hamish's, waited while I got my car, then followed me to work. He even escorted me inside. When I get there, Jo was on the phone with Reilly. She was pouting prettily, so I assumed he was telling her something she didn't want to hear. As soon as she spied Curt, she said, "Well, Curt's here to protect Merry."

Curt gave me a goodbye kiss. "Just please don't go wandering off alone. Promise?"

"Promise."

"Jolene, tell Reilly goodbye," Mac yelled. "We've got to get some work done here."

Jo pulled her phone from her ear and stared at it. She looked floored. "He said I'm not to call him again! And then he hung up on me! On me! His wife! I only called a couple of times."

"Five." Edie held up a hand with the fingers splayed.

"Six," Mac corrected. "Now get to work, all of you!"

In response to Reilly's and Mac's perceived mistreatment, Jo went on a crazed bit of deadheading, pruning and watering. Edie ignored Jo but insisted on mothering me, bringing me Coke and snacks and offering her sixteen-year-old son, Randy, as bodyguard. Larry the sports guy pontificated on all the things he'd learned from reading Tom Clancy books on the Special Forces. He obviously saw some connection between my bomb and infiltrating and exfiltrating without the enemy's being aware you'd been there, though I missed the correlation myself.

When things finally calmed down a bit, Mac beckoned to me.

I went to his desk and stared when he offered me a seat.

"Mac, are you sure? You've never done this before. Will you regret it in the morning?"

"Just sit, Kramer."

I did, grinning.

He touched his picture of Dawn with his forefinger, then looked at me. "You realize what this attack means, don't you?"

"Somebody doesn't like me? But that's okay because I don't like him very much, either."

He gave me his bored look. "It means I'm innocent. I didn't murder Martha."

"My car getting blown up proves that you're innocent?"

"Absolutely."

"Okay," I said, uncertain of his logic. Not that I thought he'd done the crime—either crime. I didn't. Then it hit me. "Is it because you like me too much to blow me up?"

He rolled his eyes. "It's because I wouldn't have failed."

I stared at him, appalled. "What?"

He let his head fall back against the headrest on his big chair. He stared at the ceiling as if beseeching the suspended tiles to give him patience. He sat up. "That was supposed to be a joke, Kramer."

"Oh. Of course."

He touched Dawn again, then grinned at me. "I have an alibi!"

Thank goodness! Then I had second thoughts. "For 3:00 a.m.?"

He nodded. "I was at the hospital with Dawn and one of her girls. And lots of people saw me."

"That's wonderful, absolutely wonderful!" And it was. What a relief! By turning in the diary, I hadn't condemned a friend to the state pen after all.

"I was at His House to pick Dawn up for a movie and just before we left, one of the girls went into labor. I drove her and Dawn to the hospital and waited for the baby to be born. It was a boy about this big." He held his hands six inches apart. "Cute little thing with lots of dark hair sticking up all over. Sort of like he'd stuck his finger in an outlet."

"So you're a dad," I teased.

He looked suddenly embarrassed, astonished and pleased all at the same time. "She said she was naming him Mac. Well, Mackenzie, but she'd call him Mac." He glanced at Dawn's picture again. "Of course, the adoptive parents will change his name, but it was the thought."

"And a wonderful thought it was." I leaned over and kissed his cheek. "Congratulations, Pop. Where are the cigars? Or the candy bars that say It's A Boy on the wrapper?"

The back door to the newsroom opened and I turned to see who had come in. William. I watched as he walked right up to Mac's desk, halting beside me.

"I take it you've heard about Merry's car," he said without preamble. I might as well have been invisible for all the attention he paid me.

Mac nodded, looking wary.

"Were you ever in the military?" William asked.

Mac stiffened. "The United States Army Reserves."

"Your specialty?"

"EOD."

"Explosives Ordnance Disposal."

Mac nodded.

"But he's got an alibi," I blurted.

Both men turned to me, but it was William who said, "Thank you, Merry. I'll talk to you later." Then he waited until my nerve broke and I turned to go.

"Merry," Mac said softly.

I looked back at him.

"It is because I like you too much to blow you up."

I felt the tears gather. I nodded and made my way to my desk.

FOURTEEN

When it was time for me to go to Mercers' to pick up Bailey shortly after one, Mac wanted to follow me.

"I don't want anything to happen to you, girl. I can't afford to lose my best reporter."

I smiled at him, understanding he meant more than just the possibility of my getting blown up, but it felt too weird having my boss tail me. "I'll be fine. Whoever it is can't do anything to me in the middle of town in the middle of the day. Besides, he can't know what kind of car I'm driving now unless he was hiding behind a tree at Mr. Hamish's or in our back lot when I pulled in. And Bailey will be with me all afternoon."

"Some protection she'll be."

"Bailey will be more than enough to keep him away. What's he going to do? Kill us both?"

He didn't look convinced. "If something happens to you, Curt will haunt me for the rest of my life. I don't even want to think about Dawn's reaction."

"You can grump all you want," I said, unmoved by

his glass-half-empty assumptions, "but I've learned your secret."

His eyes narrowed. "What secret?"

"You're a chocolate-covered cherry."

He looked appalled.

"Hard shell on the outside but soft and sweet inside."

"Please! Spread rumors like that and I might as well pack my bags and leave town."

I was grinning as I left the newsroom and went to my navy rental. As I drove to the Mercers', I started thinking about how life often juxtaposed the extraordinary, like exploding cars, with the ordinary, like teasing your boss or going on interviews. When something amazing, bizarre or astonishing happens, it seems as though there should be a break in time to enable adjustments, whether physical, emotional or spiritual, on the part of the person experiencing the overwhelming events.

But it doesn't work that way. Life continues, responsibilities remain and appointments wait. All a person could do was shrug and keep going, trusting that the Lord knew what was happening and was there to care for you.

Of course, maybe the Lord knew that doing the ordinary was the best way to cope with the painful and unexpected. Routines center reeling thoughts and feelings, giving structure to a life suddenly gone off on a strange tangent, forcing you to go forward when all you want to do is hide in bed with the covers over your head.

Bailey came down the walk in a slow, careful stride, opened the passenger door and slid in. Her glorious hair was caught at her neck in a large gold clip and her eyes were heavily rimmed with black. Her face was very pale and carefully blank, and I wondered what she thought about spending the afternoon with me and the ministry's various clients. After she buckled her seat belt, stretched as far as it would go, she sat with her hands clasped in her lap. I noticed for the first time that her nails were bitten to the quick. They were also painted black.

She was dressed in two voluminous T-shirts over her sweatpants, the shirt underneath yellow, its sleeves showing where the black sleeves of the upper shirt were rolled almost to the shoulder. The yellow hung below the black almost to her knees and I thought of night-shirts. I wondered how she could stand all those clothes in the July heat. I felt wilted in one layer of clothes, let alone two or three.

Bailey was quiet as we drove to our first interview. I wondered if she was this shy around everyone, or if it was just me. I began to doubt she'd be any great asset in the upcoming interviews. I was afraid she'd sit there scowling like Snoopy in his vulture persona, making everyone uncomfortable.

I was pleasantly surprised when she opened up as I pulled to the curb at our first stop.

"Mrs. Santiago is a widow who needed Good Hands to repair some plumbing and fix her roof," Bailey told me as we walked to the door of an old green bungalow near the edge of town. The door opened and a tiny woman with much gray streaking her short black hair smiled at us. A gold front tooth gleamed in the sunlight.

"Bailey, *mi amiga.* You get *más hermosa* every day," Mrs. Santiago said in a voice that carried the accent of her native Mexico. She leaned up to kiss Bailey's cheek. "Come on. Come in."

We followed her into a living room where a window air conditioner labored to keep the heat at bay. A floral border circled the walls about eighteen inches from the ceiling and balloon curtains made of floral sheeting that coordinated with the border hung at the windows. I knew immediately that Candy and her helpers had been involved here as well as the team that did the actual repairs.

"I was part of the crew who worked on Mrs. Santiago's house," Bailey told me, pride radiating from her like heat from the scorching pavement out front. She turned to the tiny woman bent with age and arthritis. "Will you tell Merry about how you came to contact Good Hands and what we did for you?"

Mrs. Santiago nodded. "So wonderful people. But first I get you something to eat. Sit." She indicated the worn sofa along one wall of her living room. "I be a minute."

I watched the old woman shuffle toward the back of the house and the kitchen. "Can we help?" I asked, half rising. "What can we do?"

"*Nada, chica.* I am fine."

"I'll help her." Bailey rose and followed Mrs. Santiago. In a moment she returned with a glass of iced tea in each hand. She handed one to me as Mrs. Santiago inched her way into the room with a third glass of tea and a plate of wonderful-looking goodies.

"This is *pan de dulce,*" Mrs. Santiago told me, pointing to the bread. "It is sweet. You will like it. And this is *buñeulos.*" Cinnamon and sugar flaked off the crisps and made my mouth water. "When I heard you were coming today, I made them for you."

"Thank you! They look wonderful."

She held the plate to me and it was no hardship to fill the pretty flowered napkin she gave me with her offerings.

"And you, *mjjito.*" She offered the plate to Bailey.

After she was satisfied that Bailey had enough to eat, Mrs. Santiago set down the plate on the scarred coffee table and sat in a green stuffed chair that had seen better days. Her small house was definitely in a less than desirable neighborhood, but it was neat and clean, even pretty. The iced tea was cool and flavored with mint—"I grow it in my backyard," Mrs. Santiago said—and the *pan de dulce* and *buñeulos* melted on my tongue.

"*Mi esposo* died ten years ago," she began. "The *niños* were grown and not here but in California, Florida, Texas, one even back to Mexico. With my social security I was able to eat, but there was not much more. This house that Carlos buy and keep up with such pride began to fall apart."

She clasped her hands over her heart. "It made me so sad, but what could I do? I did not know how to fix things and I did not have any dollars to hire someone. When the roof in the bedroom began to leak, I move the bed and put a pail under the leak. When there was a drought, everyone pray for rain. I pray the drought would continue. What if my roof fell in?"

I thought of the house I'd grown up in and the house Curt owned and which would become my home in another week. If there was any problem that needed fixing, both my parents and Curt had the means to get someone to do the work if they couldn't do it themselves. But Mrs. Santiago had no one and no money. She moved the bed.

Her face broke into a smile, her eyes bright. "Then my mailman tell me about Good Hands. He give me a paper one Sunday when he walk his route on his free time. 'Call them,' he tell me. 'They will help you.' But how could I call strangers?" She spread her tiny hands in question.

"Then we have a week of rain, every day, and another leak started over the bed. I put plastic over the bed and a bucket on it, but it was no good. I think I will have to move the bed to the living room when I remember the mailman's friends. I call them, and they come." She smiled. "They fix my roof. They fix everything! The ladies come and make things *muy* pretty. And they come back every year to check on me. I still have only my social security, but I have friends now. Like the *bonita* Bailey."

Bailey was still beaming when we left and I felt blessed by Mrs. Santiago's hospitality and gratitude. I just hoped the other four people we were scheduled to see didn't feed us, too. I wasn't sure I would have room.

Bailey gave a little gasp as we were getting into the car.

"Are you okay?" I asked.

"Fine," she said, her smile gone. "I stubbed my toe."

I looked at her black flip-flops, which matched her black eye makeup and today's black fingernail polish. At least her toenails were au naturel.

"You go to Faith Community Church, don't you?" Bailey asked hesitantly.

"I do. Do you?" I didn't remember ever seeing any of the Mercers at church except for the time Tug spoke.

"I do. Mom and Dad still go to our old church."

I didn't say anything, but I wondered at the wisdom of families going to separate churches.

Bailey brought a finger to her mouth and began trying to find some remaining nail to bite. "I told them I wanted to go to a church that had a larger, more active youth group. They didn't like splitting us up—they can't leave where they are because Dad's an elder—but they're so worried about me that they agreed." She smiled sadly. "Anything to help Bailey."

"They love you," I said.

"I know. And I'm very proud of them."

But it wasn't enough to help her with the unhappiness that enveloped her like a shroud.

There was a moment of silence. Then Bailey said, "You play in the bell choir, don't you?"

I nodded.

"Is it as fun as it looks?"

I grinned at her. "More. I have to really concentrate because I'm not that great a musician, but I love it. After all, you only have to read your notes and keep count. For me the notes aren't hard, but the rhythm can be very challenging."

"Do they ever have openings?"

"Sometimes." It struck me that my bells would need someone when Curt and I moved to Pittsburgh. Maybe Bailey could take my place.

"Why don't you come to practice with me tonight and see if you think you want to let Ned know you're interested?"

"Tonight?"

The more I thought about it, I more I liked the idea. Bailey would have something to look forward to, something to get involved in, and I wouldn't feel I was letting Ned and the others down when I left. Bell choir isn't like a vocal choir. If someone is missing with bells, those notes don't get covered, where in a vocal choir the rest of the section covers for the missing person.

"I could pick you up on my way," I told her. "You'd love it and maybe you could play a bit." I slowed as I approached a Stop sign. "Do you play any instruments?" It had just dawned on me that I didn't want to stick the choir with someone who wasn't competent.

"I play the piano a bit and I used to sing in the kids' choir when I was little."

Good. If she could play the multiple notes of a piano score, she could handle the bells. "Do you sing in the school choir now?"

She didn't answer immediately and I looked over at her. She was sitting stiffly and holding her breath, her lower lip caught between her teeth. Oops, touchy subject.

She let out a breath. "No, I don't. Would you mind taking me home?"

I blinked. "What about our list of people to visit?"

"You don't need me and I need to go home." She sounded strained, almost desperate.

"Sure," I said, turning to go back in the direction we'd come.

We drove in silence for a bit, then I asked, "How do you like Pastor Tom?"

"Who?"

"Pastor Tom, the high school pastor."

"Oh, him. He's very nice."

Nice wasn't usually the word people used for Tom. He was wonderful, creative, fun, super, over-the-top, a maniac—superlative words. Nice was very bland for Tom. And it clicked that she didn't know him, that she wasn't going to the youth programs either Sunday morning or any other time. No matter what she told her parents, she wasn't coming to Faith for the youth programs.

But she was coming for the main service. She had to be to know I was in the bell choir. I glanced at her, huddled miserably against the passenger door.

Lord, this kid needs Your help big-time.

FIFTEEN

When Curt and I pulled into the church parking lot for bell choir practice, the first thing I saw was Bailey getting out of a van parked by the side door to the building. She was back in all black, a men's vest worn over a black men's shirt whose tails tickled the backs of her knees. Not that they actually tickled her knees. She had on her usual sweatpants and nothing would tickle through those.

I began to sweat just looking at her. It was almost seven-thirty in the evening and the temperature was still eighty. I was wearing khaki shorts, a red T-shirt and flip-flops. At least Bailey and I agreed on casual footwear, though mine matched my shirt and had little plastic daisies all along the thongs.

"I'll be back around nine," Curt said.

"Sounds good." I gave him a kiss and climbed from the car.

I walked over to the van where I found Candy sitting in the driver's seat. She gave a little wave and leaned out her window. She indicated Bailey. "She said you said she could come. Are you sure it's all right?"

"I did, and it's fine." I grinned at Bailey. "I'm glad you made it. You must be feeling better."

She shot a quick look at her mother. "Oh, I'm feeling fine. Like always."

I nodded, knowing she was keeping something from Candy. But then didn't all teens keep things from their moms? "Don't worry about picking her up afterward, Candy. Curt and I'll bring her home."

"You sure it's no trouble? I'll be glad to come get her."

"Go home and enjoy your evening. Bailey and I are going to enjoy ours, right?"

Bailey nodded, looking hopeful for a change.

Candy left and we walked into the rehearsal room. It was ordered chaos with everyone helping with the setup of the tables, topping them with heavy foam pads to protect the bells. Over the foam went cloths to protect the foam and on them the bells were being arranged in progressive order, each ringer responsible for his or her own bells. One of my bells being middle C, I was just about smack in the center.

I didn't even have a chance to get my bells before people began rushing me. It was a bit disconcerting.

"Merry! Thank God that you're here!" Maddie Reeder, my best friend at church, grabbed me in a tight hug. "Are you all right? I've been so worried!"

I blinked and patted her back. She'd obviously heard about the car. She was shaking and I was afraid she was crying. "I'm fine, Maddie. Of course, my car's seen better days, but I'm fine."

She pulled back and searched my face. "Are you sure? When I heard, I almost died. I tried to call you all day."

"My phone was in the car," I explained. "In my purse."

"It's gone." Her voice was full of sorrow, as if it had been a living thing. "What will you do?"

She must be more upset than I thought if she didn't know the answer to that one. "Get another."

"That wasn't what I meant, and you know it."

Oh.

"What happened?" Bailey asked, eyes wide at Maddie's show of emotion.

"Her car got blown up!" Maddie said dramatically.

Bailey looked at me like I'd grown a second, make that a third, head.

"And she works for a man who's a murderer and probably an attempted murderer!" Mrs. Weldon stood just behind Maddie. She had her arms wrapped around her middle like she was cold. Mr. Weldon was beside her, nodding his head, his lone bell held in his gloved hand.

"I don't!" I said, shocked at the comments.

"Merry," Mr. Weldon said, "you've got to go someplace safe. What if he tries to blow up your car again and this time you're in it? Maybe the FBI or the CIA can put you in witness protection or something."

"What?" I stared at the Weldons aghast. Witness protection? "But I didn't witness anything."

"We don't want something bad to happen to you," he said, patting my shoulder. "We care."

"It's that Mac Carnuccio." Mrs. Weldon shook her head, her face dark with some emotion. Dislike? Concern? Anger? "He always was a bad one."

"Mrs. Weldon, don't say that, please!" My heart was racing and the chicken divan I'd made for Curt was rolling around uncomfortably in my stomach. "Mac's a nice man and a good boss. I like him. He'd never hurt anyone."

"If you say so, dear." She patted my hand, obviously having decided that my judgment had been turned by the trauma of the explosion.

"Mac hasn't been accused of anything." I tried to keep my voice level, but it was hard when I wanted to scream at her for saying something so unfounded. "And I don't think he's done anything wrong."

"I heard it was just a matter of time before they come and cart him off in cuffs." Rob Ramsey, a slim but strong man who played the biggest, deepest bells, was eager to add his information to the mix. "They've got a diary and she had that tattoo. Mac's guilty."

I went cold. "What diary? How did you hear about a diary?"

"See? I told you," Rob said to Jeni Whitman, who played the F and G to Maddie's left. "There's a diary. And Mac's name is in it."

"I didn't say that!" How had people heard? Who had leaked the information? Was William going to think it was me? "Where did you hear that, Rob?"

He frowned as if he was trying to recall. Finally he shrugged. "Everyone knows."

Several people nodded. "Yeah, everyone knows."

"Haven't you heard of innocent until proven guilty?" I demanded.

"Mac has a reputation," Jeni said, looking worried

though I wasn't sure whether she was concerned for me or for herself because she expected Mac to track her down and do her in.

"It's a long way from being a womanizer to being a murderer," I said, quoting Curt. "And besides, he has an alibi."

"Oh, my dear," said Mrs. Weldon kindly. "Don't you know that alibis can be arranged? There are always people who will say anything for money, just like the vile men at Jesus's trial."

Everyone nodded, and I thought, *Hello? Do you hear how ridiculous you all sound?* So the rich rulers paid men to give false testimony at Jesus's trial. What did that have to do with Mac? There were no rich rulers in his life, no trial, not even any legal action.

"Be sure your sins will find you out," Rob said pompously.

Thankfully at this point of the discussion, Ned clapped his hands. He was puffing and he'd deposited a tennis racket on a chair by the door. "Sorry I was late, people. Let's get to our places."

I was seething and I was scared as I took my place. As a result I had a hard time concentrating. Usually I could push everything out of my mind and focus on the bells, but the stark reality of what people were saying and thinking about Mac wouldn't stay conveniently tucked away. I was so bad that Ned finally stopped us midsong and said, "Merry, you're so off beat that you're making all of us crazy."

And you're all so off base about Mac that you're making me crazy.

"Let Bailey try my part," I said, stripping off my gloves. "I need to go to the ladies' room."

I didn't pause long enough for Ned to respond. I just marched out of the practice room and into the ladies' room. There I sat and struggled with my emotions.

These people in bell choir were nice people, but they were saying appalling things. If they were talking like this, what about the rest of the town? Was everyone ready to hang Mac? For the first time I understood why certain trials were moved to new venues. If jurors were selected from the choir tonight, they would all be prejudiced against Mac, even Maddie.

My eyes filled with tears. I would have expected better of her.

But, I reminded myself, she and all the others were only repeating what they had heard somewhere. The real issue was, where had these rumors originated, especially about the diary? That was supposed to be a secret known only to the police and the person who dropped it. And me. I knew I hadn't told anyone, even Curt. Certainly William hadn't. So who?

Oh, Lord, how did this gossip get started? And what should I do about it?

And what should I do about Mac? As I thought about him and prayed for wisdom, I realized that there was nothing I could do for or about him short of finding the murderer. Like I had a chance to actually do that. It seemed nothing less would clear his name.

Oh, Lord, I give Mac to You. Please take care of him and clear his name.

Ten minutes later, I walked back into the practice room, calmer for having put Mac in God's hands.

Bailey was reluctant to give up the bells, which I considered a good sign for the future. I wasn't sure I wanted to play with these people anymore, anyway. Let her fill my slot.

I slid my protective gloves back on and checked my music to see where we were. I picked up my bells. Then I looked at everyone in the line of bells, finishing with Ned standing in front of us. Some looked back at me and some stared at their music rather than meet my eye.

"I apologize for throwing things off tonight, Ned," I said. "I was just taken by surprise by what people were saying about my boss. I like him and I trust him. I ask that all of you—" and here I looked up and down the line again "—not jump to conclusions based on hearsay. I also ask that you pray for him. It's a very difficult time for him, especially if he knows what people are saying. I've been praying about Mac's relationship with the Lord for some time and he seems to be showing an increasing interest. I would hate to think that anything we at Faith Community Church did would keep him from truly knowing Jesus." I took a deep breath. "I'm ready, Ned."

For the rest of practice I was able to concentrate, but I was exhausted by the effort when we finished. We were all putting our bells back on their cases when Maddie said loudly enough for everyone to hear, though she was looking at me, "Merry, Doug and I want to invite you and Curt to come to dinner Saturday night. I'll give Mac and Dawn a call and ask them, too."

"Really?" I looked at her and knew she was taking a step of faith based on my belief in Mac. "We'd love to come. It sounds like a great evening." I leaned close to her and whispered, "You're wonderful, girlfriend. I knew you wouldn't fail me."

She gave me an understanding smile. "That's what friends are for."

"How did Bailey do?" I asked, looking over at the girl. She sat at the upright piano in the corner, moving her hands back and forth above the keys as if she were playing some phantom melody.

"Very well." Maddie grinned. "You'd better watch it or she'll put you out of a job."

Little did Maddie know.

Suddenly Bailey's phantom music became real as she gave in to the temptation to actually play. Notes rippled and flowed, danced and raced, tiptoed and thundered. Everyone stopped whatever they were doing, astonished by the glorious music coming from the nail-bitten fingers of the awkward girl who no longer looked awkward but graceful as her hands chased each other across the keys.

"She told me she played a little bit of piano," I muttered to Maddie.

"She's wonderful!" Maddie began clapping, as did everyone else when as suddenly as she began, Bailey stopped. She sat, head bowed, body tense, teeth gripping her lower lip. Slowly she rose, face pale, eyes full of burdens I couldn't imagine.

I put my arm around her and Curt and I took her home.

SIXTEEN

Police drove past my place all night, their lights making patterns on the ceiling of my bedroom as they passed. I hoped they weren't keeping Mrs. Anderson awake, but I did feel safe even if I couldn't sleep soundly. I kept picturing the burning car and reeling with the thought that I'd almost died.

Early Friday morning William showed up with one of the bomb squad men, and they went over my rental car thoroughly before they let me near it.

"It's clean, Merry," William said. "You're good to go."

"You're sure?"

The bomb guy grinned at my hesitance, held out his hand for the keys, and climbed in the car. The engine turned over smoothly.

"There you go," he said, holding the door for me.

Curt drove into the lot just as the cop shut my door. He climbed out of his car, leaned in my window and gave me a good-morning kiss.

"You've got circles under your eyes," I said.

"Couldn't sleep. I kept having this recurring nightmare."

"Yeah, me, too." I waved goodbye to William and the bomb cop. "You can't come with me now, you know."

"I know, but I can at least see you get there safely."

So we drove in a small parade to Primrose Bridal Salon where I had an appointment for the final fitting of my wedding gown. I rang the bell as Leslie Ingles had told me since the salon didn't open for another hour and a half. As I waited for her to let me in, I waved goodbye to Curt, who was reluctantly pulling out of the lot.

In spite of yesterday's traumas, I felt like turning cartwheels. One week from tonight was our rehearsal dinner. One week from tomorrow I'd become Merrileigh Carlyle, Mrs. Curt Carlyle. I said the name over and over in my mind. Sweet.

Leslie waved at me through the plate glass door as she unlocked it. She reminded me of a sparrow, hopping busily from project to project, her energy never flagging.

"I'm all ready for you," she said. "Your gown's in the fitting room and it's so beautiful. Go on in and I'll be right there. I want to get the coffee and sweet rolls."

I went into the fitting room and there it was, hanging on a hanger, the loveliest thing I'd ever owned, the loveliest thing I'd probably ever own. Mom had come to visit shortly after Curt and I got engaged and we'd gone shopping with Jolene, Maddie and Dawn.

Maddie, Mom, Dawn and I all said, "Yes!" as soon as we saw this dress, but Jo had held out for more bling.

"Sorry, Jo, but I'm more Charlize Theron than Cher, more grace than glitz."

"What's wrong with glitz?" she demanded, looking down at her rhinestone-studded jeans. "And I'm graceful."

"Yes, you are," Mom said diplomatically. "You're beautiful and you wear glitz and bling with great panache. However—" she smiled lovingly at me "—Merrileigh is tailored in taste." She glanced at my head. "Except her hair."

Mom still hadn't recovered from when I'd chopped off my hair, almost as long as Bailey's, though not as gorgeous. It had been almost a year, but then she didn't get to see me every day and hadn't gotten used to my spiky appearance.

"And I have no idea what we're going to put on your head," Mom said with a worried frown.

"Ah," said Leslie, "I do. That's why you pay me the big bucks."

And she produced the perfect veil. Even Jo had to admit it looked great.

Now Leslie bustled in with the food and drink and set them on a counter well away from the gown and the raised fitting stand. Then she helped me lower the gown over my head and did me up in the back. Then she stepped away and let me stare.

I looked elegant. I never look elegant. I couldn't stop smiling.

Sheer fabric covered my arms and shoulders,

joining the silk in a straight line above the bodice, which was row after row of tiny horizontal pleats. The skirt fell softly with only a hint of my shoes showing and it swished as I turned this way and that before the three-way mirror. Seed pearls and Swarovski crystals twirled and twined about the hem. I loved the way the slight train would catch up into a bustle after the ceremony.

"Here." Leslie held out my long veil, which fell from a circle of flowers touched lightly with seed pearls and Swarovski crystals like those on my gown. She fastened it in place. I grinned at my reflection. I might not be bridal-magazine beautiful, but I thought Curt would be impressed when he saw me.

I hated taking the dress off. Maybe if I called Curt, he'd grab Pastor Hal and we could do the deed today. We'd had our blood tests and had the license already in hand. I grinned when I thought of what my parents' reaction would be to that.

"Are you crazy, Merry?" Dad would yell. "All that money down the drain!"

"Don't worry about it, Phil," my mom would say. "We're still having the party. After all, Merry doesn't want to give back all those wonderful gifts."

I grinned, thinking of them.

Lord, let us move to Pittsburgh so I can be near my family, not North Carolina, where I'd be even farther.

Curt and I would wait until next weekend for the wedding and all it signified, just as we'd planned, and not because of the gifts. We wanted our friends and family with us and, besides, I wasn't rebel enough to flout expectations. My brother didn't call me Marshmallow Merry for nothing.

Leslie put the dress on its padded hanger and swathed it in protective sheeting and plastic. The dress wouldn't dare get dirty after all that care.

"You look absolutely wonderful in this," Leslie said as she laid the veil in a box, using sheets and sheets of tissue paper to keep it from wrinkling.

I knew she said that to all her brides and it was probably true of them all. Still, it was good to hear.

"Make sure you keep them away from that cat of yours," Leslie said as she carried the veil's box out to the car.

As I followed her with the gown held in my arms like a lover might carry his beloved, I didn't even regret the huge hole in my savings account that it represented. Sometimes the outrageous expense was worth it.

I drove straight home where I hung the gown on the back of my bedroom closet door and laid the veil box on the dining room table, the only flat space besides the kitchen counter long enough to hold it.

When I finally made it to work, I was still humming a happy tune. The tune soured somewhat as I opened my e-mail and almost immediately received an instant message from Tony Compton asking for another meeting "to make the information in the article as full and compelling as could be." He suggested meeting in the afternoon at four or, better yet, the evening at six.

I'll treat you to dinner for your kindness. You pick the restaurant.

I had too much to do in the office to meet in the

afternoon, though I was tempted to take him up on the dinner suggestion and select the most outlandishly expensive place I could think of. The thought fled immediately. I knew there was no way I wanted another dinner with him. Besides, I was planning on moving more of my stuff to Curt's.

Can't do this afternoon or tonight, I IMed back. How about Monday?

3:30? he suggested.

It's a date. I cringed as soon as I sent it. That's what happens when your fingers fly faster than your brain.

A date? Then let's make it 6:30, and we'll talk over dinner.

3:30 it is, I typed, wanting to add an exclamation mark but knowing that was overkill. And unprofessional. Monday, 3:30. And I hit Send and signed off as fast as I could. I sat back in my chair and stared at my screen. Tony was charming, but he was also pushy. And I wasn't going to be pushed. I stamped a metaphorical foot for emphasis.

Jolene eyed me. "What's wrong?"

"Nothing."

"Hah. You, Miss Perky, look ready to snarl."

"Miss Perky?" Now I really wanted to snarl. "Perky rhymes with turkey, you know."

She looked at me like I was crazy.

"Perky is like cute," I said. "You're supposed to outgrow both."

"Well, I hate to tell you this, but you're definitely both." She looked at me with her typical smugness.

"Perky as a black-eyed Susan and as terminally cute as Johnny-jump-ups."

Great. Now I was flowers.

Her eyes lit up as a new thought crossed her amazing mind. "By the way, your wedding bouquet will look absolutely beautiful." She and Reilly had insisted they assume responsibility and costs for all the wedding flowers. As Reilly put it, "It's our thanks for all you did for us when Jo was in such danger last winter. And flowers are Jo's thing."

I had agreed when I realized how important it was to them. I knew the expense wouldn't make a dent in their resources and Jo did know flowers.

"No bling, remember?" I could see my bouquet dripping with rhinestone-encrusted streamers and feathers.

"No bling, but wonderful color. I'm taking Friday off and Reilly and I are going to the flower mart in Philly to get everything we need. You'll love it!"

I would. Her taste in clothes might be a bit overwhelming at times, but she was a genius with flowers. "Thank you so much. I know it'll all be beautiful."

She looked humbly at her feet; her royal purple toenails matched her fingernails which matched the purple capris and the sequins splashed across her lavender top.

"But," I said, "no purple nail polish at the wedding."

Jo looked at me in disbelief. "Our dresses are coral. No way would I be gauche enough to wear purple with coral."

"That is a great relief," I said as I grabbed my purse.

Jo glanced quickly at Mac, hunched over his desk. "Are you having your weekly lunch with Dawn?"

I nodded.

"Sergeant Poole was here again this morning before you got in." My stomach, which had been looking forward to lunch, suddenly soured. "I'm scared for him, Merry."

"Yeah, me, too." And she didn't even know about the diary. "People are talking, saying all kinds of terrible things. But he's got an alibi for the car thing."

"Innocent people get set up all the time," she said.

Maybe not all the time, but it did happen.

She glanced at Mac again. "I asked him if he had an alibi for Martha's killing."

"And he said?" I already knew the answer.

"No."

Of course not. If he had one, he'd be off the police's radar. Thank goodness he had one for my car.

"He said he slept alone the night before the killing, got up and ate alone and came into work early. He saw no one and no one saw him." She wrinkled her nose. "Almost seems too bad that he's dating Dawn."

"What?" Talk about a non sequitor.

"You know what I mean."

And given a minute to think, I did. Back in the old days, Mac would probably have slept with whomever he was dating and thus he'd have an alibi. But Dawn held firm to the scripture that taught chastity outside marriage and consequently Mac had slept alone in his own bed.

Jo's cell rang and as she reached into her purse for it, she said, "Tell Dawn I'm thinking of her and Mac and praying for them."

I hid my surprise at the praying-for-them comment and said, "I will. Thanks."

As I walked to Ferretti's to meet Dawn, I didn't know what to expect. I hadn't talked to her since the murder, so I didn't know what she knew or how she felt about what she knew. Was Mac being a murder suspect enough to kill their romance?

She was waiting for me, dark circles under her eyes. As I slid into my seat, she yawned.

"Sorry," she mumbled from behind her hand. "I've been at the hospital since 3:00 a.m. I came here from there. Second night in a row."

"Mac told me about the first one." I grinned as I remembered his face when he said the mom was naming the baby after him.

"He was so cute," she said, her eyes warming. "So proud."

Proud I could buy. But cute? Mac? If ever a man had outgrown cute, it was Mac. Talk about the eye of the beholder.

"Tell me about last night."

"She had two, a set of fraternal twins, a boy and a girl. The little girl was a complete surprise to all of us."

"Is she going to keep them or put them up for adoption?"

Dawn shook her head and covered another yawn. "I've got to get something to eat before I fall over! And I don't know. She doesn't know. She's only been with us a couple of weeks and she's spent most of that time refusing to listen to anything I or any of the counselors say."

Astrid appeared.

"Still no new server?" I said.

Looking disgruntled, she shook her head. "My feet

are killing me. I'm not used to being on them all day. I got a stool behind the reception desk so's I can take a load off. No time for taking loads off working tables."

As soon as she disappeared with our orders, Dawn leaned in. "So how's he doing?"

I knew she meant Mac. "It's hard to tell. He sits at his desk barking out orders as usual, but he's got to be feeling the strain. I understand Sergeant Poole was in again this morning to talk with him." I eyed her. "How do you think he's doing?"

Dawn began making concentric circles on the table with her iced-tea glass. "He won't talk with me about it. He says, 'I don't want to drag you down into my dirt.'"

"Oh, boy. He's trying to be noble."

"But I don't want noble." Her voice was fierce. "I thought we were way beyond noble. I thought we had gotten to sharing."

Oh, Mac, you're going to ruin it if you're not careful.

"Dawn, look at it from his point of view. To him you are the quintessential good girl, and he is the clichéd bad boy. For some reason he has fallen for you, probably against his better judgment, and to his surprise you've returned the favor. When things were moving at their natural pace between you, he could deal with the little steps, the one-at-a-time issues. But now things are anything but normal and he feels he has to protect you from his wild past and the complications it's caused."

Dawn rubbed her temple as if she had a headache brewing. "I spent last night in the hospital with a seventeen-year-old who had twins without benefit of marriage. One was white, the other mixed race. She'd had no prenatal care at all. None. She was riddled with venereal disease—active open sores—and she wasn't with us long enough for the doctor to make delivery safe. My heart breaks for the problems these babies might face as a result."

Talk about the sins of the parents being visited on the next generation.

"I do not live in an ivory tower or a cloister," Dawn said emphatically. "I know the score. Just because I'm a virgin doesn't mean I don't know about life. I probably know more about the seamier parts of it than he does, seen more of the dead-end lives that come from it. And if my own work weren't enough, my dad ran a rescue mission for years in downtown New York back when Times Square was corrupt and vile, an open sewer of sin."

"Have you told him all this?"

"Repeatedly, but he doesn't seem to get it. He certainly doesn't get forgiveness, either mine or God's."

"He's got you on a pedestal."

"I don't want to be on a pedestal. I want to be a partner." She all but snarled it.

"You two look like you're having a happy conversation."

We both turned and found Mac standing beside our booth. He had his hands in his Dockers pockets, trying to look nonchalant. I hoped he didn't notice all the people at the other tables staring surreptitiously at him.

Guilty until proven innocent.

SEVENTEEN

Dawn slid over on her bench seat and Mac slid in beside her.

She looked at him. "We were talking about you."

"Oh." He sighed, then glanced around at all the people who quickly averted their eyes. "Well, so is everyone else."

Poor Mac. He was all too aware of what people were thinking and he looked miserable—and fearful?

He gave Dawn a sickly grin, no match at all for his usual cocky one. "I figured you'd be here with Merry and I just stopped to say hi." He cleared his throat nervously and grabbed Dawn's iced tea. He took a long pull on her straw. She picked the glass up as soon as he put it down and took a lengthy sip herself.

He stared at her and I wondered if he'd gotten her subtle I-care-for-you-we-even-share-germs message. I thought maybe he had until he said, "Well, I'd better get back to the newsroom." He started to slide from the booth.

My heart broke a bit to see hard-nosed, brash,

cynical Mac afraid he was going to lose the woman he had come to love. Not that he was, but he thought he might. It was a very painful way to come to terms with the consequences of past actions.

Dawn grabbed his hand in both of hers. "Don't you dare leave."

He sat, expression uncertain and painfully hopeful. Dawn kept a firm grip on him, leaning into him, lowering her head to his shoulder briefly.

"I was just telling Merry that you're driving me crazy," she said when she straightened.

He gave her a half smile and with his free hand traced the circles under her eyes.

"Another night in the delivery room," she said.

He nodded. "Everything go all right?"

"Twins. One mixed-race boy. One white girl."

He blinked. "Same mother?"

Dawn nodded. By now they were clasping hands and leaning toward each other. "That's reminds me of an issue I want to talk with you about," she said.

They'd forgotten I was there, so I grabbed my purse and walked to the cashier. "Tell Astrid I'll take my BLT to go."

I ate at my desk, thinking how strange life was and praying that Mac would understand the totality of God's forgiveness. When Jo came back from her lunch with Edie, they demanded I tell them all about my lunch with Dawn. Well, Jolene demanded and Edie nodded approval. I gave them an expurgated version, telling them how tired Dawn looked and why as well as telling how people were watching Mac. All I said about

Dawn's and my conversation was that Dawn was on our side in believing in Mac's innocence.

"Yes!" Jo pumped the air.

Edie smiled. "I knew she was a good woman."

At two I left to visit Fenton Strickland, one of the largest corporate sponsors of Good Hands. Over the past thirty years Mr. Strickland had built his architectural firm from one employee—"Me, working from our basement"—to more than fifty in three Chester County locations.

"At first we gave money and encouraged our people to help Good Hands for PR reasons. It made Strickland Architecture look good. Then I realized that the teams of Strickland employees who helped Good Hands on 'our' days had this common bond that carried back to work. There was a camaraderie created in sweating together while painting or roofing or repairing leaks."

Mr. Strickland grinned and fiddled with the knot of his tie. I'd noticed that all the men in this office wore ties and the women dresses or pantsuits. Professional though not pompous was my assessment.

Mr. Strickland angled his head to indicate all the people outside his office. "They especially liked seeing me in a Strickland T-shirt getting every bit as grubby as they were."

What was it about seeing the boss in a parity situation that so pleased employees?

"Some of our employees began bringing their teens to help and I started bringing my son Chaz. A lot of the teen–parent tension between him and me disappeared as we hammered and sanded together."

Interesting, I thought. Maybe I should talk to Chaz. Get his take on things.

Mr. Strickland leaned forward, suddenly intent. "Though all the reasons I've mentioned are important, it finally dawned on me that the reason to help Good Hands is very simple. It's the right thing to do."

I stood and thanked him for talking with me. "You've given me exactly what I want."

"Would you like to take a picture of all the personnel here who have worked with Good Hands?" he asked.

"That'd be great." I usually avoided large group photos because they had to be sized down so much for the paper that you couldn't see the individuals. Still, there was no way I could say no to this suggestion. The use of the picture would be up to Mac.

I leaned over and pulled my camera out of my purse. When I straightened, Mr. Strickland's dress shirt and tie were gone, and he was wearing a gray T-shirt with Strickland Architecture in crimson letters. He turned around and on the back were the words "dirty hands make Good Hands."

I was laughing as I walked out of his office and saw that several men had shed their dress shirts and ties and were wearing their T-shirts. The women had pulled their shirts on over their dresses or blouses. They quickly gathered outside in front of a large evergreen.

I clicked several pictures and pulled out my notebook to get names when one of the women handed me a neatly typed sheet with all the names in the right order.

"We decided to be ready just in case," Mr. Strickland

said as he walked me to my car. "We planned it all yesterday. Good team building, you know."

"And not bad PR," I said with a smile.

He grinned back. "Absolutely."

I smiled all the way back to the office where I spent the rest of the afternoon entering the interview and all the employee names into the story file, and speaking to other sponsors on the phone. All in all, a good day.

When I pulled into my parking space after work, I met Mrs. Anderson climbing out of her car.

"Hello, dear," she said. "A week from tomorrow." And she grinned.

I grinned back.

This evening she was wearing a smart royal blue pantsuit with white sandals and purse. Her makeup was nicely done and her hair was neatly combed, though the purple streaks at her temples were still evident. Her injured arm was now in a sling made of a scarf that coordinated with her pantsuit. She sparkled with spirit and joie de vivre.

We walked past the lilac together and I looked at my palm. The orange of the antiseptic they'd painted me with had almost disappeared.

"Have you ever been to the Elizabethan Tearoom?" Mrs. Anderson asked.

I shook my head.

"Oh, my dear." She laid a hand on my arm. "You must go some day for high tea. It's wonderful! Little party sandwiches, scones with clotted cream, pastries including the most wonderful meringues. You'd absolutely love it! Why, I feel like I won't have to eat again until your reception." She patted her convex tummy with satisfaction.

A meow interrupted us.

I glanced up and there sat Whiskers on the living room windowsill. He often sat there, watching the birds, salivating as if he were thinking about what he could do if someone just gave him the chance. Usually he sat there on the inside. Now he sat on the outside.

"Baby!" I hurried toward him and he stood, meowing for me. He leaped into my arms. "What are you doing out here?" I stroked him, trying to calm him. "You're okay now. You're okay."

Mrs. Anderson scratched him behind the ears and under the chin with her good hand. "How long has he been out here? I didn't see him when I left to meet my friends for tea."

I was certain he had been inside when I left the apartment this morning. For all his grandiose plans for lowering the bird population, he didn't like it much outside. The grass felt funny under his house-soft pads, and other creatures live outside, some quite big and canine. The wind blew, ruffling his fur and unnerving him.

Maybe he'd somehow gotten out when I was bringing in my wedding gown. I'd left the door open while I hung the dress and while I went back to the car for the veil box. I didn't recall checking to see that he was inside before I left.

Thinking about my wedding gown made it shimmer before my eyes and the mystery of Whiskers' escape dimmed.

"Mrs. Anderson, would you like to see my wedding gown? I brought it home this morning."

It was probably bad luck to show it to someone ahead of time—or was that just for the groom seeing the bride on their wedding day? And who cared?

Mrs. Anderson's face glowed. "Oh, Merry, what a treat! I'd love to see it."

I fished my keys from my purse and unlocked my front door, my only door. I pushed it open. Whiskers shifted in my arms, and I hesitated before stepping in. What if someone had been here when Mrs. Anderson and I were both gone and that was when Whiskers had gotten out? With all that had happened recently, I couldn't discount that possibility, could I? My reluctance could be wisdom or paranoia. I preferred to think of it as wisdom.

I stuck my head in and looked right and left. Everything looked normal though something smelled strange. I wrinkled my nose. Looking straight ahead through the dining room into the kitchen, I could see something shining on the counter. Broken glass. The window directly above was broken, but there were no jagged shards caught in the frame like there would be if a neighborhood kid had thrown a ball through. The frame had been scraped clear. Then I noticed the hair standing up on Whiskers's back. He knew something was wrong, too.

Knowing I was probably making a fool of myself but past caring, I turned and ran, grabbing Mrs. Anderson's good arm and dragging her with me.

"What's wrong?" she asked as we burst off the porch.

"I don't know," I yelled as I propelled her into the yard. I was heading for shelter behind the lilac tree when a horrendous crack of sound tore the air and a great gust of wind knocked us off our feet. Again.

EIGHTEEN

I sat on the sofa in Maddie and Doug Reeder's living room, Whiskers in my lap, and felt the tears wetting my face though I wasn't making any noise. I was beyond noise.

My apartment had been blown up and I had almost been blown up with it. I hadn't been, but everything that I hadn't yet taken to Curt's had been.

"My wedding gown!" I blurted again. "My wedding gown!" That beautiful dress that made me look elegant. That glorious veil that fell from a circle of flowers that allowed my spiky hair to spike as usual.

"It's okay, honey." Curt tightened his arm around me. "I'd be happy to marry you in a burlap bag."

I abandoned my misery for a moment to pull back and glare at him.

He looked startled. "What?"

"You don't understand!"

"I guess I'm too busy being grateful you're still alive to worry about some dress."

"Some dress? Some dress? It was my wedding gown!"

Maddie hurried into the room. "Holly's finally down for the night." Six-month-old Holly was the light of Maddie and Doug's lives.

Maddie came over and knelt in front of me. She took my hands in hers. "Are you sure you're all right?"

I nodded miserably. Physically, I was fine. A couple of bruises from hitting the ground too hard, but that was it. Mrs. Anderson was all right, too, though her lovely blue pantsuit would never see use again. She was at her daughter's, being loved just like I was.

"I lost that beautiful picture of Curt's and my joined hands that he painted for me for Christmas."

She nodded, her eyes teary on my behalf.

"I didn't want to take it off the wall. I loved looking at it and wasn't going to take it to his house—our house—until Thursday. Then I was going to hang it in the bedroom." A huge sob caught in my throat. "It's gone."

"I'll paint you another, sweetheart." Curt kissed the top of my head. "Don't you worry about it."

I nodded and patted his knee. "Thanks." I knew he meant well, but it wouldn't be the same. That picture represented the turning point for him, the moment when he became willing to risk loving me in spite of his history of loss. The replacement wouldn't mean the same thing. I sniffed and blinked. Maddie was a blur.

"And my wedding gown, Maddie! My wedding gown!" My nose was so stuffed I could hardly breathe.

"Merry, no! I was so relieved when I thought it was still at the Primrose."

"Uh-uh. I had my final fitting today and brought it

home. It was hanging on the bedroom door." My voice had risen several octaves by the time I was finished.

Maddie made a horrified noise of total understanding and I threw myself into her arms.

"Honey, it's okay," Curt said, patting my back. "We'll just get you another."

"It won't be the same," I sobbed, my nose choosing this moment to start running. I pulled back before I soaked Maddie's shoulder. "Tissues." I held out my hand.

Maddie slapped a box in my hand. "Don't try to understand, Curt. It's a girl thing."

"A piece of advice, buddy," Doug offered from his observation seat in the leather recliner across the room. "You have to determine if she wants advice, I'll-fix-it-for-you words or just sympathy. Hands down, this is sympathy time."

Curt sat still for a moment, processing those astounding words. Then he pulled me close and began rubbing my back. "I'm so sorry, honey. I'm so sorry."

Maddie patted my knee and stood. "Your guy's got great possibilities, Mer. And you—" she walked to Doug and climbed in his lap "—you did very well."

We sat quietly for a few minutes. I don't know what the others were thinking, but I was thanking the Lord for the people He'd put in my life since my move to Amhearst.

Then the phone played the opening bars of "Finlandia" and the doorbell rang. For the next couple of hours there were calls that Doug handled and visitors who Maddie welcomed. I sat on the sofa with Curt and tried to be gracious, though I had become so sleepy I could hardly keep my eyes open. Too much crying.

At ten o'clock Maddie opened the door to my parents and Sam, and I ran into their arms. The four of us stood in what we used to call a huggle, a combination hug and huddle, while I cried again.

"Thank you for being here for her," Dad said to Curt when we finally broke apart. He grabbed Curt's hand and shook it. I was surprised to see tears in Dad's eyes.

Then he turned to me. "All right, Merrileigh. What's going on here?"

We sat down and I told him everything that had happened.

"But we have no idea why!" I finished.

"So you lost everything at the apartment."

I nodded. "Thankfully I'd taken some of my things to Curt's already."

"At least your wedding gown's safe at the shop," Mom said.

Teary-eyed all over again, I shook my head.

Mom looked wonderfully horrified. "It's gone?"

I nodded. "Gone."

"Oh, Merry!" Her cry was full of anguish.

"Now, Barb," Dad said. "We'll get her another. It'll be all right. You'll see."

Mom and I both glared at him and he got that what-did-I-say look.

"Mars and Venus, Dad," Sam said. "Though I have no idea why. Personally, I thought that was a good suggestion."

"I think, Mr. Kramer," Curt said, "they don't want fix-it lines. They want commiseration."

Mom looked at Curt with approval. "Oh, Merry, this one's definitely a keeper."

I smiled. He was. And Pittsburgh looked closer than ever.

By midnight I was tucked away in the guest room of Maddie and Doug's home. Mom, Dad and Sam had gone home with Curt. I wasn't sure I'd sleep, but after a couple of false starts, I wasn't aware of anything until sunlight falling across my face woke me. I stared at the ceiling for a few blinks, trying to remember where I was and why. When I remembered, I heaved a huge sigh. So much gone. And whoever was doing this would probably try to hurt me again.

Hurt you? Get a grip, Kramer. Kill you.

I shuddered. If I lay there and thought about my situation any longer, I'd expire from fear and save my unknown enemy the trouble. Forget that. If he wanted me gone, he was going to have to do it himself.

Action. Movement. That's what I needed. I sat up and reached for the phone by the bed. I called Leslie at the Primrose Salon.

"I heard last night," she said when I identified myself. "Jolene called. We've been on the Internet all night looking for another gown just like yours. I have a couple of possibilities and so does she. Looks like the best bet is one Jolene found. It will be shipped from the UK first thing Monday."

I was going to have a wedding gown from England?

"It will arrive here late Wednesday. I'll fit it on

Thursday and have it ready for you by late Friday afternoon even if I have to stay up all night. So relax. You'll be just the bride you wanted to be."

After offering my profuse thanks, I hung up, amazed and weepy, but this time the tears were happy ones.

Curt, Mom, Dad and Sam came over for breakfast and Maddie made delicious French toast with just a hint of cinnamon. Holly, all blond curls and blue eyes, sat in her high chair and made google eyes at Sam, who appeared smitten back.

"A girl could do worse," I told Holly as I smiled at my little brother who was now more than six feet tall.

"In about ten years you can have one of your own," Dad said to Sam, forkful of toast halfway to his mouth. "That way you'll have your college loans paid off before you get stuck with a mortgage."

Sam looked horrified, whether at the idea of babies or mortgages I wasn't sure. "I think I'll just wait twenty years for Holly to grow up." He reached over and chucked the baby under the chin. "Right, sweetie?"

She grinned so broadly that the mouthful of stewed peaches Maddie had just shoveled in dribbled out and down her chin.

Sam frowned at her. "In the meantime you can work on your table manners, okay?"

Holly beat happily on her high chair tray with a spoon.

I was struck by how normal everything seemed, yet how weird.

We weren't nearly as cheery a group a half hour later as we stood in a semicircle in the parking area of my apartment and looked at my rental and Mrs.

Anderson's spiffy red car. I should say, formerly spiffy. Both vehicles were scorched and had windows knocked out, whether by the heat of the blaze or flying debris at the time of the explosion, I didn't know.

Curt glanced at me with a quick grin. "Poor Mr. Hamish. Another car bites the dust."

Poor Mr. Hamish indeed. He and I had a long history in which I destroyed the cars he rented me. "It's a wonder the man even speaks to me."

"He thinks you're fascinating." Curt squeezed my shoulders. "Me, too," he whispered.

We took the front walk past the lilac, its leaves curled and brown at the edges from the heat of the fire. Then we stood outside what was left of my apartment. The building stood, but my half was pretty much gutted. The feelings of loss and violation were so strong that I had to swallow repeatedly to stay in control.

Why is this happening to me, Lord? And why now?

Yellow crime-scene tape sagged under the intense heat of the sun. Smoke and the rank odor of wet charcoal hung in the humid air. I pressed against Curt and he held me close.

"At least most of my honeymoon clothes are in a suitcase at your house," I said.

He nodded. "I wish I could tuck you away there, too."

"Only a week," I said, but those seven days stretched out like forever. A terrible thought struck me. "What if I bring this trouble with me? What if something happens to your house? To your paintings? To you?"

He shrugged. "Just so nothing happens to you."

As we stared at the mess, two questions filled all our minds. Who and why?

"You must have seen something when you found that girl," Sam said.

"I've been over it a million times. I didn't see a thing. And Jolene was with me. No one's going after her."

NINETEEN

Now that they were sure I was all right, Mom and Dad and Sam left midafternoon to go back to Pittsburgh.

"We'll be back at the end of the week for the wedding," Mom said as she kissed me goodbye. "Curt, you take care of her for us." She gave him a fierce glare, and he quickly nodded agreement.

She must have been satisfied, because her pique reared its unattractive head. "I still have a hard time getting my mind around the fact that you're getting married. It's probably because I didn't have much to do with the planning." She smiled bravely as Dad darted her a cautionary look. I don't know whether she saw him, but she said nothing else.

Poor Mom. She was disappointed that the wedding was to be here in Amhearst rather than back home, but she had been very good about keeping her opinion to herself, at least most of the time, a fact that both Curt and I appreciated. I knew she felt cheated that she hadn't gotten to do much of anything in the preparations. Mom loved to organize and what better thing to organize than your daughter's wedding?

I knew she felt I was robbing her of one of life's privileges, an admirable attitude considering the complaining I'd heard her friends do about the headache of getting their daughters' or sons' weddings together.

Curt and I had chosen to have a small wedding in Amhearst for several reasons. We'd met here. Our mutual friends were here. And since Curt had no family, his parents and sister having died, I wanted him to be where he felt comfortable, not the outsider.

"We love you, sweetheart." Mom kissed me goodbye.

"Love you, too," I said.

"And you, too, Curt." Mom gave him a hug and a buss on the cheek. "Keep her safe, you hear?"

Curt slung an arm over my shoulders. "I will."

"We're counting on you, son," Dad said as he climbed behind the wheel.

"No pressure, though," I assured him as we waved them out of sight.

"Yeah, right." He hugged me. "Come on. Let's go for a ride. I want you to myself for a while."

We drove south out of town, meandering along the winding roads to Doe Run, enjoying the scenery, the animals in the fields and each other. Eventually we rounded a curve on one of the back roads, and there sat a covered bridge spanning a sturdy stream.

I was charmed. "I've seen the bridge over on Harmony Hill Road in Downingtown, but this one's so pretty out here in the countryside." Its sides were painted barn-red and its roof wore gray shingles. We drove through it on a continuation of the macadam road, the roof momentarily shutting out the sun, the sides blocking our view of the softly undulating fields all around. Openings high in the walls just below the roof line allowed for air to circulate.

"It should be raining rather than sunny so we can take protection from the elements," I said, thinking about the past generations of buggies, wagons, riders and animals who had sheltered here, waiting for a storm to pass. "Beep your horn."

Curt hit the horn and the honk was wonderfully resonant in the confines.

"The keeping out of the elements had a downside to it," he said. "In the old days when it snowed and people traveled by sleigh, they had to shovel snow into the bridges so the sleighs could pass over them."

I laughed. "There's a catch to everything, isn't there? Bet they never thought of that when they were building the bridges in high summer."

When we'd passed through, Curt pulled to the side of the road. "They didn't really cover the bridges to protect the people and animals," he said. "They did it to lengthen the life of the bridge itself. It must work. This one was built in 1881."

"Over one hundred and twenty-five years old." I swiveled in my seat and looked back. "Impressive, though I'm sure there's been much repair work done since back then. And why are we stopping?"

Not that I minded. Open fields spread out on either side in a green carpet. White daisies and wild mustard bloomed in profusion and a Louisiana blue heron, disturbed in his search for fish by our arrival or maybe our horn blowing, took off from the stream, huge wings thrumming the air, slender neck retracted, long legs trailing behind.

Curt reached onto the backseat and picked up a camera. "I'm doing a series of paintings of the covered bridges of Chester County. I like to photograph them so I get all the details right."

I followed him as he walked down the road and took several shots of the bridge head-on. Around us honey bees buzzed from yellow flower to yellow mustard flower, and pollen floated in the air. Honeysuckle grew along the verge of the road, its scent a sweet perfume in the warm air. Red-winged blackbirds perched on reeds that looked too slight to hold their weight. A fat groundhog looked at us over his shoulder, then waddled away, his fur shimmying over his well-rounded rump. In a distant field, a pair of horses stood nose to tail, idly flicking away the flies. The silence was deep and comforting.

Next we climbed over the fieldstone approaches to the bridge and Curt took shots of it on an angle. Personally I thought this vantage point would be wonderful for a painting with the wedge of field in the foreground and a few wildflowers thrown in for color, then the red bridge and behind it the vivid green trees set against the brilliant blue of a summer sky, a strategic cloud thrown in for good measure.

Next we made our way down to the stream, where Curt took several shots of the supports of the bridge.

"They're like stilts set in concrete pads," I said, but

bridge supports didn't really interest me. I stood on a rock and stared down into the run, watching the water flow on its way to the— "Where does this stream flow? Into the Brandywine Creek?"

"Probably. Then the Schuylkill River, the Delaware River, Chesapeake Bay and finally the Atlantic."

"Busy stream." On the far side of the bridge my eye was caught by a cluster of raspberry brambles draped over the stone approach. Suddenly my mouth watered for raspberries.

"Come on." Curt took my hand and pulled me along the stream away from the bridge and the raspberries. Every few steps he glanced back but didn't stop until he was satisfied. I turned and saw why. The full span of the bridge was visible with the stream curving beneath it. Curt shot several more pictures.

We started to walk back toward the bridge and my eyes went to the raspberries again. I pointed. "Let's pick some raspberries."

"Sure." He tucked the camera in his shirt pocket, then sat on a rock and took off his sandals. He stood, tucked them in his shorts at the small of his back, and stepped into the water. "What are you waiting for?"

I pulled my sandals off and followed him. The water was cool on my feet, but it felt good, relaxing, cleansing. Here with only the occasional caw of a blackbird, the burble of the brook and the murmur of insects, I felt far removed from the trauma of the last few days.

The water inched its way to my knees, wetting the bottoms of my cropped pants, but I didn't care. It was sunny and hot and they would dry in no time. We reached the other side and clambered up the slight incline to the raspberry patch. Sure enough, red fruit waited for us. We picked carefully, watching out for thorns, and popped the fruit into our mouths. It was sweet and tart, its seeds and flesh a fascinating contrast.

When we had stripped the patch, we returned to the stream and dangled our hands in the water to wash away the sticky juice. The tackiness that wanted to glue my fingers together disappeared, but the red stains didn't. I held my hands up for Curt to see. "Caught redhanded again."

He held up equally stained hands. "At least we're a matched pair."

Laughing, delighted to be together, we waded across to the side where we were parked. As I climbed out and sat to put my sandals back on, I said, "We should have brought a picnic."

Curt dropped beside me, our shoulders touching. "Another day. I need to come back again to get pictures in the rich light of approaching evening as opposed to the harsher light of midday."

I looked around. "Will we be here to come back? We'll be in Pittsburgh."

"Or North Carolina."

I fixed my eyes on the bridge. "Tony Compton said he'd move to Pittsburgh for me if he were my fiancé. There is always room for another good lawyer in such a town, he said."

Curt leaned back, supporting his weight on his elbows. "Thinking about trading me in, are you?" He didn't sound too worried about the possibility.

I turned and wrapped my arms around his waist. "No," I said, resting my head on his shoulder. "I'm not in love with him."

We stayed like that for a few minutes, wrapped in each other's arms in the middle of a beautiful meadow by a historic bridge and a burbling rill, and I wondered how we were ever going to resolve our dilemma. I thought again of the people who had sheltered in the bridge or sledded through. They probably didn't have to face two job offers, lucky them.

"I'm going to fly down and visit the art institute Tuesday," Curt said and kissed the top of my head. "I'll be back Wednesday."

"What?" I pulled away from him and stared. And what was with the kiss on the head as he made the grand announcement? Was it supposed to make me feel better somehow?

His eyes were bright and excited behind his lenses. "They've made all kinds of arrangements for me to meet everyone from the president of the school on down. I'll get to see the facility firsthand and learn how they see me fitting into the picture. I'll see the area, look for places we might live and learn what the benefits of moving there would be for us."

"You're going to North Carolina?" I couldn't believe it. I probably sounded as distressed as the fiancées in the early 1940s when they said, "You're going to the South Pacific?"

"Merry, I'm not going to the moon. It's a short flight. And you can come with me if you want."

I didn't want.

"Maybe if you see it, you'll like it."

"I don't have any vacation time left. I'm using it all and more for our honeymoon." I was glad for a legitimate excuse not to go. I wasn't interested in seeing the place, in liking the place. I tried to ignore the little voice that tried to tell me I was being just a tad immature here. But I'd been praying so hard about Pittsburgh, I couldn't believe he hadn't caved yet.

"Sweetheart, I've got to check this out. How can we make choices if we don't know anything about one of the possibilities."

But North Carolina's not a possibility! "You don't understand. I have to let Mr. Henrey know by Tuesday."

Curt shrugged. "You'll have to tell him you need more time. If he really wants you, he'll give it."

"What do you mean, if he wants me? Of course he wants me. That's why he called." I heard my anger and took a deep breath. "Sorry."

Curt took my hand. "Merry, I know you want to go home, but I'm not sure that's a good place for us to start our marriage."

I stared at him. "You're kidding. How could it be bad?"

"It's not that it would be bad. It's more that starting off somewhere where we're both in the same position seems wiser. If we go south, neither of us would know anyone. There'd be no family to worry about, no old friends to keep introducing me to."

I glared. "First off, you would know all the people you met during your interviews, so you would know people."

"That's not what I meant."

I ignored him. "And why do you think we'd have to worry about family? My family would never interfere."

"That's not what I meant, either."

"And I won't introduce you to anyone. I promise."

He looked at me, jaw set. "I'm going."

The drive back to Maddie and Doug's was silent.

TWENTY

"Can you get that, Merry?" Maddie asked when the doorbell sounded. She and I were in the kitchen putting some last-minute touches on our dinner.

"Sure," I said with false enthusiasm, hurrying to the front hall. I had been trying to act all happy and bride-to-be-ish when I really felt cold inside after Curt's and my standoff, and I was relieved to have at least a moment without pretense. I let my smile fall away and my shoulders sag. I don't do disagreement well.

Doug was upstairs bathing Holly, washing off all the residue of her dinner. I could hear her splashing and gurgling happily.

Well, at least someone's happy today, I thought miserably.

"Yo, girlfriend," Doug suddenly said, his deep voice floating down the stairs. "You're the one who's supposed to be getting the bath, not me."

Holly's answer was another loud splash and a string of excited nonsense words. I couldn't help smiling in spite of my lousy mood.

I opened the front door to find Dawn and Mac on the porch and Curt pulling into the drive. I welcomed Dawn with a kiss and Mac with a hug. He looked uncomfortable, his dark brows drawn together in a frown. Doug and Maddie were Dawn's friends from church, and though Mac had met them when he'd come to church with Dawn, they were essentially only acquaintances. Given the suspicions and doubts he knew many harbored about him, he must wonder why they'd chosen to invite him over for the first time now.

Dawn looked at Mac with exasperation. "Merry, tell this man that Maddie and Doug aren't trying to show how liberal minded they are by having a suspected murderer in their house. Tell him they're just nice people having friends over for dinner."

I didn't think either Mac or Dawn wanted to hear about the comments at bell choir, so I was glad I could say with truth, "Maddie and Doug are nice people, Mac. Just come in and enjoy."

"No hidden agendas?" he asked, obviously unconvinced. "You're sure?"

"Aside from suspending you over a vat of acid and sticking you with an electric cattle prod until you confess?" I blinked big innocent eyes at him.

He sent me his patented you-are-so-ridiculous-I-won't-deign-to-comment look.

"Get in here." I grabbed his arm and hauled him through the door as Maddie came hurrying from the kitchen to welcome them. The three of them walked toward the back of the house while I waited on the front porch for Curt. I watched him stride up the walk, my smile gone.

He stopped at the edge of the porch, the one step down making us almost eye level. We just stared at each other for a minute. I felt tears building and tried to blink them away, but he saw them and put a hand against my cheek. I leaned into his hand and we stood like that a moment.

Then he pulled me to him and kissed me, a hard, possessive kiss that made my heart leap and my eyes tear again.

When we came up for air, I buried my face in the side of his neck. "I'm sorry," I mumbled. "I'm sorry."

He rested his head on mine. "I know, sweetheart. Me, too."

That we would be in such disagreement over where to live astonished me. I knew it was naive of me, but I had thought we'd never find ourselves on different sides of anything that really mattered, that we would be different from other couples. But we weren't. "What are we going to do?"

"I don't know, but we'll figure it out somehow." He stepped away. "I just hadn't realized how stubborn you are."

I frowned for a beat until I saw the teasing light in his eyes. Then I slugged him lightly in the chest. "Me? Look who's talking."

He smiled softly. "I love you, Merry."

"I know. I love you, too."

This time the kiss was gentle and sweet.

A high-pitched gurgle behind me made me turn. Doug stood in the doorway with rosy-from-her-bath

Holly wearing her diaper and a onesie covered with animals. She held her pudgy arms out to me, talking a blue streak as I took her.

"Hey, precious," I whispered and blew a raspberry against her neck. She giggled and batted at me. She smelled of baby powder and love.

"Give me a kiss," I said.

She leaned in and placed her open mouth on my cheek. She hadn't yet gotten the smacking part of a kiss down.

"Now Uncle Curt."

He bent and she gave him the same wet kiss. When she straightened, she looked so proud of herself that we all laughed at her. She laughed back, delighted with herself and life.

Feeling much better than I had for several hours, I followed Doug and Curt into the backyard. Holly sat in her high chair on the back deck and gummed pretzel sticks while we ate the steaks, Vidalia onion slices and red, yellow and orange bell peppers that Doug had grilled, as well as the potato salad and from-scratch baked beans Maddie had made. By the time Holly rubbed her sleepy eyes with her grubby hands, she was almost as messy as she'd been before her bath. Doug and Maddie excused themselves to put her down.

Mac, who hadn't joined in the conversation very much, followed them inside with his eyes. "You were right, Merry. They are nice folks. Still, I think it's open-minded of them to be willing to have dinner with a murder suspect."

I shook my head at him. Mac was often purposely provocative, but I hadn't heard him sound so bitter in a long time. One thing for sure, it certainly strained the relaxed feel the evening had had to this point.

Dawn turned to him, frowning. "Stop it, Mac. No verbal sparring or poor-me games tonight. You didn't kill anyone and we all know it."

He looked at her, one eyebrow raised in challenge. "Maybe not, but I've done everything else."

Listening to them, I had the feeling that with Doug and Maddie gone, Mac felt free to continue a discussion that he and Dawn had been having earlier.

Dawn snorted. "Like I haven't heard that line before. Give me a break."

"And you." He glared at her, but I noticed he kept his arm along the back of her chair, his fingers resting lightly on her shoulder, his fingers fiddling with her hair. "You're pure as the driven snow." He made it an accusation.

Dawn glowered at him. "Don't be ridiculous."

"You are." He looked at Curt and me. "Right? Is she not the quintessential good girl?"

Dawn showed a lot more patience with him than I would have. "Any goodness I have is only because of Jesus."

I nodded agreement, but he wasn't interested in what I was thinking. He was intent on Dawn once again.

"That's too easy an answer," he said. "Too pat. Too simplistic."

"Tell it to God," Dawn said. "Not me. He's the One who sent Jesus to die for our mistakes and wrongs, yours, mine, everyone's."

"Yeah, well, I've made too many mistakes and wrongs."

"Never." She reached up and caught his hand where

it rested on her shoulder. "Never, Mac. You can't out-sin God's forgiveness."

We sat in silence for a few minutes. I looked at this intense, driven man who for years had used wild living to still his inner demons. "Women and whiskey," he used to say with a satisfied smile. "Broads and booze."

Now he saw the folly of such behavior. Now he saw faith and love in action in Dawn and recognized the difference between "fun" and real joy, but for some reason he still considered himself a pariah.

"Mac," I said, "you're a newsman. Telling the story and telling the truth are what you do for a living. You gather facts, analyze them, arrange them. Often they're unpalatable or uncomfortable and you can't imagine how the politician could have been so foolish or the murderer so cruel. But it's truth. It's what really happened. You don't flinch from printing it. Why do you flinch, maybe even turn away, from the truth of God's love and forgiveness?"

He stared at me for a moment, his expression the strangest mix of hope and hopelessness. Then he jumped and grabbed for his vibrating phone. He glanced at the readout, then rose. "Excuse me."

As he walked a few steps away, I smiled at Dawn. She smiled wanly back.

"He can be so ornery and cantankerous," she said, "but it's all a cover for that inner sensitivity, that inner vulnerability that tells him that he's been so bad for so long that God can't possibly want him."

Mac as a sensitive man was an interesting if slightly world-tilting-on-its-axis thought. I had to agree with him that he did have much for God to forgive. When I met him, his reputation screamed *wild man* and he made sure his actions confirmed it. Strangely, in the middle of all his riotous living, he was somehow taken with Dawn and what she stood for. When he finally got the courage to ask her for a date, he was floored when she accepted—if he went to church with her.

"Why would she go out with someone like me?" he had asked.

Good question. All I knew was that his lifestyle changed at that time. The more enamored he became with Dawn, the more he tried to please her. Since Dawn wasn't about to compromise her high standards and Christian commitment, it meant Mac had to conform to her way of life: no more sleepovers; no more nights in smoky bars flirting and drinking, hitting on the pretty girls; no more hangovers or lost weekends.

Not that she demanded the changes of him. She didn't. She just kept being the woman she'd always been. Her problem was that she had fallen as hard for him as he had for her. Since she believed that a believer should only marry another believer, she too was caught in a quandary of emotion versus conviction.

"Yes!" Mac yelled as he rushed back to the picnic table. "Come on, Kramer! They're bringing in Ken Mackey!"

TWENTY-ONE

Ken Mackey walked into police headquarters under his own steam, accompanied by his parents, his older brother, Elton, and Tony Compton, his new lawyer. Ken ignored everyone; Elton nodded to Mac; Tony smiled at me.

Then Tony broke from the group and walked over to me. He took my hands in his. "Are you all right?" he asked with flattering concern. "I've been so worried about you."

Slightly embarrassed because everyone was staring at this little side drama, I said, "I'm fine, Tony. Really."

"If you say so." Then he glanced down and saw my red hand. His head came up. "You are hurt."

"No." I blushed. "It's raspberry stains." All around me reporters were watching and writing. A TV crew was taping.

"Are the police taking care of you?" Tony asked.

"I've got a twenty-four-hour watch," I said. "Friends." I indicated Mac.

Tony looked startled. Because he thought Mac was still a suspect? "Well, tell them they can count me in to help," he said. "I mean it."

"Thanks. I will." Maybe.

With a nod, he hurried back to his client and family waiting at the door.

Tony laid a hand on Ken and muttered something to him. Ken nodded. The entire party turned and faced the news media present. Not only were we there, but the *Daily Local News* from West Chester, the *Main Line Times* from Devon, the local stringer for *The Philadelphia Inquirer* and a couple of TV crews circled the steps.

Tony pulled out a piece of paper and read, "Ken Mackey has come to speak with the police of his own volition. He has been out of town for several weeks competing. As you all know, he is a nationally ranked motocross rider. He extends his deepest condolences to the family of Martha Colby, feels grief himself at the loss of a good friend and looks forward to this conversation with the authorities to help them in any way he can to find the person responsible for this heinous act. Thank you."

Tony then reached into the briefcase he had left on the steps when he came to speak with me and pulled out a sheaf of papers. "Here are copies of our statement for all of you." He handed the papers to the nearest person, who in turn passed them on. Mac and I each took a copy as the papers made their way to us. We passed them to the *Daily Local* woman.

With a nod to all of us, Tony turned, as did the Mackeys, and went inside the station.

"Well, that was anticlimactic," I said as Mac and I climbed back in the car.

"But important." He frowned. "If Ken was out of town at competitions, he'll be cleared easily."

I glanced at him. "Mrs. Wilson saw two people at Martha's. She named Ken and the new boyfriend."

"So she did, but she is eighty-three years old."

I gave a humorless laugh. "Don't let her age throw you. She's sharp as a tack."

"Maybe mentally. What about her eyesight?"

I had to admit that was a good question and one I hadn't considered. "Well, if it wasn't Ken, assuming the dates of his competitions check out, which I'm sure they will, who was it? And who in the world is the new boyfriend? After all, he's been around since April and here it is, the end of July. Someone must have seen him."

Mac looked at me. "How do you know he's been around since April?"

I experienced a brain freeze, pain and all, just like I did when I ate something cold too quickly. "Uh," I said, totally lacking Mrs. Wilson's mental acuity. How did I explain knowledge I only had because I'd read Martha's diary, something I wasn't allowed to mention to anyone?

We were turning into the street where Doug and Maddie lived. "Almost home," I said brightly.

"What is it about you, Merry?" Mac looked at me like I had just flown in from some outer galaxy. "I can't get William to tell me stuff like that."

Relief surged through me. "It must be my feminine wiles."

"You? Wiles?" Mac started to laugh, the first genuine

laugh I'd heard from him since Martha's death. It was so good to hear him laugh I didn't even mind that it was at my expense.

We were almost at the Reeders' when I grabbed Mac's arm, making him swerve. "Did you see that?"

"Watch it, Merry!" He just missed swiping the fender of a car parked on the street.

"Did you see?" I repeated, pointing to Maddie and Doug's.

"What?" He still sounded miffed.

"A dark shadow."

He glanced all around. "It's pushing eleven at night. There are dark shadows all over the place."

"Not running through Doug and Maddie's yard."

He hit the brake, actually stopping right in the middle of the street. "You saw someone running across the Reeders' yard?"

I nodded, wrapping my arms about myself. "I'm sure of it." For the first time in my life I wished I suffered from paranoia. Then I could blame the vision on an unruly imagination.

"Tall? Short? Man? Woman?" Mac demanded.

I shook my head. "Just a dark shadow wearing black." I rubbed the goose bumps on my arms as I had a terrible thought. "Do you think someone put a bomb in Curt's car? Or attached something to the foundation of Maddie and Doug's house?"

Once again I felt the heat from the explosions I'd experienced, the force of the blast as I was blown off my feet. I always came back to the same question. What had I done to make someone try multiple times to kill me?

Mac looked grim. "We'll check the car, believe me, though I'm not too worried about the house. Too many innocent people there."

I hoped he was right. "Don't you guys check the car." The thought of Curt or Mac getting blown up made me shudder. "Call the police and get the bomb squad."

Mac took his foot off the brake and we rolled slowly into the drive. Curt had had to move his car for Mac to get out for the news conference and it was parked in front of Maddie and Doug's garage. We pulled in directly behind it.

"Mac, the front porch light is off and so is the lamppost beside the drive."

I could see Mac frown in the weak light of the digital readouts on the car's front panel.

"They were on when we left," I said. "I'm sure of it."

"They were," he agreed.

"The dark shadow doused them, maybe so no one would see him working on the car." Now my goose bumps had goose bumps and my heart was pounding.

"What have you done to make someone so determined to get rid of you?" Mac asked as we climbed out of the car.

"I don't know." My voice sounded shaky. I took a deep breath. I would not cry from fear or frustration. "I've tried to think of something, anything, but I can't." Certainly articles about the Coatesville city council or West Chester University's latest budget issues or Amhearst's school board woes didn't engender the type of emotion that led to murder. Verbal defamation perhaps, if the feelings were strong enough, but not the taking of a life.

"It's got to be related to Martha's death," Mac said as we walked up the dark path, trying not to trip on the cracks between the pavers. "You've been involved from the get-go."

"But Jolene has been, too, and no one's trying to blow her up."

In the silence that followed this comment we heard a weak meowing sound.

"Cat," I said, glancing up and down the street, looking for some stray amid the shadows.

"I bet that's what you saw. A cat, scurrying across the yard."

Mac liked that idea a lot and I couldn't blame him. It was much more palatable than a person planting another bomb.

"Not a cat unless he's clever enough to run on two feet. It was a person, Mac."

We stepped onto the porch and the meowing noise sounded closer but still weak and wobbly. "Maybe there isn't a bomb at all. Maybe it was someone dropping off a litter of kittens he didn't want." I bent to peek under the azalea bushes that grew against the house.

I heard Mac make a surprised *argh* kind of noise.

"What?" I turned in time to see him go down on one knee.

"Get some light out here! Quick!"

All my fear came rushing back. Booby traps! Bombs. Death. I began beating on the door. "Curt! Help!" I stopped my hand on its way to the door for another slam. "Is it safe for them to open the door? We're not going to blow up the house and us, are we?"

"Hardly." He stood with something in his arms. The weak mewing started again.

The inside door flew open and Curt appeared looking frantic, Maddie, Dawn and Doug right behind him.

"Merry! What's wrong?" He threw open the screen door and grabbed me. "Are you okay?"

"I'm fine. Really." I was thrilled as he pulled me close and wrapped his arms around me.

"You scared me out of another one or two of my nine lives," he said. "But what's wrong?"

"Mac," I said. "Kittens." I pointed as he stepped into the light spilling from the front hall.

But it was no kitten Mac held in his arms. It was a baby, all red-faced and wizened and bleating weakly.

TWENTY-TWO

We stared in disbelief at the bundle in Mac's arms. A baby!

Dawn recovered first and pushed Curt and me aside to get to Mac. She pulled him inside under the hall light.

"It's a newborn," she said. "Only a couple of hours old."

Since she saw newborns all the time including two just this week, I knew she knew what she was talking about.

Deftly she took the baby from Mac and went into the living room. She sat on the sofa with the rest of us crowding around and Mac collapsing beside her. She opened the soft yellow hand-knit blanket that was loosely wrapped about the child. Skinny arms and legs with skin so translucent that the veins showed moved weakly. A little T-shirt and the smallest diaper I'd ever seen covered the baby's body.

"Do you have a cotton baby blanket?" Dawn asked Maddie as she checked the baby for the requisite number of fingers and toes and looked in that tiny diaper to determine sex.

"Coming right up." Maddie hurried upstairs.

As Dawn worked, a note slid out of the folds of the yellow blanket and fell to the floor. Doug picked it up.

In surprise he said, "It's for you, Merry."

"Me?"

He held it out and I could see my name printed on the front of the envelope. I took the missive and tore it open. I scanned the note, only a few lines, and gasped.

"Read it," Curt said. Everyone nodded.

I cleared my throat. "Merry, please take care of Elise for me. I'm trusting her to you because you are a good and kind person."

I looked at the baby flailing in Dawn's lap. I was supposed to assume care of this child? Me? "I can't take over care of a baby just like that! I'm getting married in a week. Besides, I don't know anything about babies."

Maddie hurried in with the cotton blanket. Dawn lifted the baby, laid the blanket on her lap, then set the baby on it. With a minimum of fuss, she wrapped the baby snugly in the blanket, little legs bent against her tiny body, delicate arms bent across chest. When Dawn was finished, the baby looked like a papoose. Dawn picked her up and cradled her next to her heart.

I glanced at Mac to see how he took Dawn's maternal actions and caught the most infatuated look I think I've ever seen.

"That's pretty much how they wrap the babies in the hospital," Dawn said. "The babies have been curled up in utero and too much body freedom is disconcerting to them."

"Elise," I said. "She's a little girl."

"Look what else was on the porch." Doug walked into the room with a large grocery bag in his arms. I hadn't even realized he'd left. He set the bag on the coffee table and began to unload it. He pulled out a small collection of baby products—two bottles, several cans of formula, baby powder, skin cream, a pacifier, a lovely soft green hand-knit sweater and a box of newborn disposable diapers.

Elise began her weak cry again.

"She's probably hungry," Dawn said. "When I'm with the kids in the hospital, they often bring the babies to nurse only a short time after birth."

"I'll get a bottle ready," Maddie said.

I looked at Dawn holding the baby so competently and at Maddie off to get a bottle ready. "She actually wants me, the least competent, to take care of this little one?"

"You can't, you know," Mac said. "There are all kinds of legal and even criminal issues here."

I nodded. "I know. I was just thinking that the mom wasn't thinking."

"I'd assume it's some young girl who is scared to death and has been for months," Dawn said.

I nodded. "She's kept her pregnancy a secret, hasn't she?"

"Probably."

"We've got to call the police," Mac said, reaching out a finger and tracing Elise's downy head. She had hair so fair she looked bald.

Dawn smiled at Mac and held Elise to him. Without a second thought, he took her.

"Marco Antonio Carnuccio, you are a wonder," she said, leaning against him.

"No wonder about it. A large family with lots of nieces and nephews," he said, smiling at Dawn, then Elise.

"And you're everyone's favorite uncle," I said, enjoying the tender side of Mac that he never showed in the newsroom.

He shrugged, which told me I was right.

"She really needs to go to the hospital," Maddie said as she handed Elise's bottle to Mac. "When Holly was born, they checked her over so carefully. I bet this little one hasn't had any medical attention at all."

"Why don't we call the police and tell them to meet us at the hospital?" Curt suggested. "That'll save some time."

Doug nodded and picked up the phone.

"Don't, Doug," I said, putting a hand on his arm. "Don't call the cops."

"Merry." Curt took me by the shoulders. "Sweetheart." He looked so serious. "You—we can't keep this baby."

I put my hands on his shoulders. "Don't worry. I know. It's just that I don't want the mom to have to deal with all the legal ramifications of abandoning her baby. I think we can avoid that whole mess for her."

He looked at me for a minute. "You know whose baby this is."

"I do."

"And you just want to give her back?"

"I do."

"But she wanted to throw her away. How can you trust Elise to her?"

"She didn't want to throw her away. Look at all the trouble she went to to prepare for her arrival." I indicated the supplies on the coffee table. I picked up the little green sweater and the yellow blanket. "She knit these for Elise. She named her. She cared and cared deeply."

"Then why didn't she keep her?"

"I don't know all those answers, though I can guess at some. Shame. Fear."

"Fear of what?" Curt asked. "Of her parents? Would we be sending this baby back into a home situation that would be intolerable?"

"We could adopt her," Maddie said, her eyes hungry as she looked at Elise. "We adopted Holly. A sister for her would be wonderful."

"Maddie!" Doug looked flabbergasted at the idea. "Holly's only six months old."

Maddie shrugged. "If people can do twins and triplets, we can do two babies close in age. Besides, it would be a couple of months before she'd be released by children's services, anyway."

"Which is all moot," I said. "Elise was left to me to take care of and I say we take her back to her mother. That girl can't go through life with the guilt of abandoning her baby weighing her down."

Curt studied me. "You know the parents, right?"

I nodded.

"And you trust them to be there for her?"

"I do."

"In that case, I agree with taking her back. I think

she needs to be held accountable. She may choose to keep Elise or give her up for adoption—and we'll suggest you be first in line if that's her choice, Maddie—but she needs to face what has happened and make a deliberate and wholesome choice from strength, not fear. Trying to ignore unpleasant things, hard things, doesn't work. I learned that with my sister. If we'd stepped up for Joan instead of not wanting to believe the unbearable, she might still be alive." He began loading the baby supplies back into the paper bag.

Mac had Elise on his shoulder, one large hand firmly spread along her small spine, supporting her from head to bottom, the other gently making circles. She gave a very unladylike, thoroughly wonderful burp. With a laugh I reached for her.

It felt like she weighed nothing as I snuggled her against me. Curt and I started for the door.

"Wait a minute," Doug said and we turned to him. "Let's pray about this."

We gathered in a circle holding hands except for my left hand in which I held Elise. Curt looped his right arm around my shoulders so the circle was unbroken. I was grateful for Doug's suggestion of prayer and took great comfort in seeking God's help and wisdom.

"Oh, Father, there's a terrified girl out there, heart-sick and lonely," he said. "Be with her. May she turn to You for comfort. Be with Merry and Curt as they take Elise home. May she be accepted with love and may all wrong and hurtful actions be forgiven as Christ has forgiven us."

We drove across town in silence, Elise asleep in my arms. I felt remarkably calm considering the circumstances, but I was convinced that keeping Elise and her mother out of the legal system would benefit both of them.

Oh, Lord, if I'm wrong, if I'm missing something, please show me quickly.

When we turned the corner near our destination, we saw an ambulance, lights flashing, pulled up in front of a house.

"Is that where we're going?" Curt asked.

"It is," I said, not surprised that a new mother with no medical help, skulking about town, would end up needing emergency care. A pair of EMTs exited the house with a gurney between them. A third EMT followed, carrying equipment. Behind him came three very scared people. It was evident in their body language and their faces.

I climbed out of the car and hurried forward. I arrived at the ambulance just as the EMTs did. They looked at me, telling me without words to get out of their way. I ignored them and moved closer.

"Hello," I said softly to the sobbing girl on the gurney.

"Merry!" She was clearly startled to see me. Then I saw hope take root as she saw the bundle in my arms. "Is that—"

"It is," I said. I felt the rest of her family move up behind me. "She needs to go to the hospital for a good checkup. Why doesn't she ride with you."

I leaned forward and laid Elise in her mother's arms.

I heard a woman's voice say, "I knew it. Oh, honey, you should have told us!"

I kissed mother and child on their foreheads. "Love her, Bailey, but do it right, okay? She deserves that much."

Then Curt and I walked away hand in hand.

TWENTY-THREE

Sunday afternoon Curt and I went to the hospital and took the elevator up to maternity. I carried a large gift bag full of sleepers in ever increasing sizes from 0–3 months to 24 months, all in girlie colors and with girlie things embroidered on them. My favorite was a pretty pink 6–9 month one with a pointed collar like a jester's, each point with a rose pom-pom on the end. My hope was that it would make Bailey laugh because I imagined she'd been crying for a long time.

My stomach jumped with nerves as we approached Bailey's door. What if she was furious with me for bringing Elise back? I knew that her secret would have come out the moment a doctor saw her in the emergency room and the revelation had been only minutes away when we arrived at the Mercers' and saw her being loaded into the ambulance.

Over and over through the night I'd reviewed what we'd done. Time and again I knew I'd make the same choice if I had it to do over again. If I hadn't known who the mother was, if I hadn't known the caliber of the family, things would have been different. I'd have called the police and turned the baby over to protective services.

But I'd known who the mother was and I knew her heart would weep forever over the choice she'd thought she wanted to make. I believe in adoption; I've seen the joy Holly brings Maddie and Doug. But Karyn, Holly's mother, had chosen from strength, not desperation. She'd acted responsibly, not clandestinely or illegally.

And then there was the expression of joy and relief on Bailey's face when I'd placed Elise in her arms.

We stood outside Bailey's door and my throat so ached with anxiety that I could barely swallow. I looked at Curt and he smiled encouragement.

"I wish this was next Sunday," I said. "We'd be in our cabin in Olympic National Park watching the Pacific roll in."

He eyed me with his version of a leer. He wasn't very good at it, but I appreciated the attempt. "Well, that's where we'll be, but are you sure that's what we'll be doing?"

"Curt!" I slugged him softly, then started to giggle. Suddenly I felt a lot better.

"Now go on." He gave me a gentle push. "I'll be waiting for you out here."

Bailry lay in bed with her eyes closed. A vase full of flowers sat on her windowsill and a bouquet of congratulatory balloons was tied to the foot of her bed. I was impressed and pleased at how fast someone had responded to her situation. No matter how bad the circumstances, a first baby is a first baby and deserves to be celebrated. I'd learned that from Dawn and the girls at His House.

On the far side of the bed was a warming crib and in it lay Elise, sleeping soundly. I tiptoed over and stared down at her. Her fuzzy blond hair was covered with a tiny pink cotton knit cap and she was wrapped papoose style in a pink cotton blanket.

I reached out a finger and ran it down her soft cheek.

Lord, her beginnings have been rocky, but I ask You to make of her a woman with a heart for God. And help Bailey figure out where things go from here.

"Hi," said a weak voice laced with uncertainty.

I looked at Bailey and smiled. "She's wonderful, isn't she?"

Bailey looked at her daughter and tears filled her eyes. All she could do was nod.

I walked around the bed and took the recliner pulled close. The hospital had designed the maternity parlor with a couple in mind and the chair I took was for the new dad so he could spend the night with his wife and new child.

No new dad smiled proudly here. How sad.

"How are you doing?" I asked. "Are they taking good care of you?"

She looked awful, pale, weary, sad. Her hair was pulled back and held loosely in a rubber band that allowed it to be pulled over her shoulder so she could lie back in comfort. Her eyes were bloodshot from crying and her nose was red.

I took the hand that was near me, the one with no IVs. She grabbed and held on so hard it hurt.

"I'm sorry," she sobbed, trying to be quiet because of the sleeping baby. "I'm sorry! Oh, God, I'm sorry!"

The last was a prayer from a broken heart.

I moved to the edge of the bed and pushed loose hair back from her wet face, my heart breaking for her. Sure, she'd created the mess she was in, but that didn't prevent me from feeling her misery. It didn't stop me from wishing I could make it better even though I knew I couldn't.

"Shh, honey, don't cry," I said. "Somehow it'll all get straightened out."

"Will it?" She groped for the tissue box on her night table. I got it and held it to her. She grabbed a fistful and mopped at her streaming face, a futile effort given the intensity of her sobs. "I don't know how I ever got in this mess. I mean, I know, but I can't believe it. And she's so wonderful!" She looked at her daughter as her breath came in quick jerks and her nose ran.

"Can I hold her?" I asked, more to give Bailey time to regain control than anything else.

She nodded as she buried her face in the tissues. I suspected that she was thinking, as I was, that she had wanted me to hold her for life.

I lifted the infant out of her crib and sat back in the recliner with her cradled near my heart.

Bailey gave a long, wobbly sigh. "Sorry. I'm bound to run out of tears sometime soon. Dehydration is just around the corner." She gave a little sad smile.

"It's all right. You have every right to cry. Life is very complicated right now."

She gave a harsh little laugh. "Complicated. That's

a nice way of putting it. I'd say it's ruined. My life, Elise's life, my parents' lives."

"I don't see how Elise ruins your parents' lives. Complicates them, sure, but ruins?"

"Makes them grandparents about ten years too soon. Puts pressure and responsibility on them they shouldn't have. Makes them ashamed of me instead of proud." Her voice caught on the last word; it was just a whisper.

"You don't think your parents love you enough to be there for you and Elise?"

"Of course they love me. They're wonderful. But they have to look good to people so that Good Hands can be successful."

"Did they tell you that?" I'd be very disappointed if I'd read Tug and Candy that wrong.

She shook her head. "They'd never say anything like that, but that's the way it is. I've r-ruined Good Hands!"

Elise jumped at Bailey's desolate cry and Bailey threw her hand across her mouth. We both waited to see if the baby'd waken. After a bit of moving about, she stilled and slept on.

I took Bailey's hand again. "Honey, I want you to listen to me. Good Hands does not depend on you or your behavior. It's a huge, wonderful God thing, not a Tug and Candy Mercer thing. It depends on the time and commitment of hundreds of men and women who want to help others. Sure, some may wonder why your mom and dad didn't keep a better eye on their kid. Were they too busy helping others to give her the time she needed?"

"Yes, yes! That's what they'll think and that's not

true. It was all my fault. That's why I tried to keep it from them. From everybody. So life could go on as usual. So Good Hands would go on as usual."

"But people who know them will know that they did their best with you. They'll understand that kids have minds of their own. And, believe it or not, most of the people who work with Good Hands won't even know about Elise."

She blinked, startled at this idea.

"She's dominating your life, Bailey, but that doesn't mean she's dominating the lives of others."

I put the gift bag on the bed.

Bailey looked at it, a genuine smile sliding briefly over her face. "For me?"

"For you and Elise."

One by one she pulled out the sleepers, tearing the tissue paper off each and holding the little garment up to ooh and aah over it. She laughed at the jester suit as I'd hoped, holding it up so the sleeping Elise could see it.

"You'll look so cute in this one, Elise. We'll take your picture in it and when you grow up, we'll show it to all your boyfriends so they can see how dorky but adorable you looked."

I laughed. "Well, that'll be better than the standard naked baby on a blanket picture. Definitely less embarrassing."

When all the sleepers were strewn about the bed and the bag was empty, Bailey held out her arms. I slid Elise into them and began collecting all the tissue paper, jamming it into the wastebasket. As I folded the little sleepers and put them back in the bag, I watched Bailey slide the baby's cap off and run her finger gently over the blond peach fuzz. She bent and kissed the top of her daughter's head.

"I can't believe I tried to give her away," she whispered. "I love her so much." She started to cry again. "How could any mother just abandon her baby like that? It just proves what a terrible person I am."

I shook my head. "It proves what a desperate person you were."

"I was that, all right. I still am, sort of. Do I keep her? Do I give her up for adoption? I don't know if I could stand to give her up a second time. But at least I'm not all alone anymore. I've got Mom and Dad now."

"How are they doing with everything?"

"As good as, I guess. When Mom's not crying, she's holding her, talking to her. Loving her. She wants the baby to call her Grandy because it rhymes with Candy. I mean, how lame is that?"

I had to laugh at her mortified expression.

"Dad has this I've-been-shot look, though he's been so nice. I think he's having a harder time than Mom."

"Women seem to automatically respond to babies, so it probably is easier for your mom. But dads—" I thought about my father and how he'd have reacted if something like this had happened to me. "Dads have a hard time with the idea that their sweet baby girl went to bed with some stupid, hormonally crazed boy. It tears their guts out."

She nodded. "Except Chaz wasn't stupid. He knew exactly what he was doing. I was the stupid one. It was done before I even realized what was happening! How's that for being an idiot?"

I looked at her skeptically.

"Yeah, yeah," she said. "You can't imagine how anyone could be quite that dumb. Well, me, neither, let me tell you. I knew all about guy-girl stuff. I even knew I wanted to be a virgin when I got married."

She opened the front of Elise's blanket and placed her forefinger against the palm of the baby's hand. Immediately the little fist closed over her finger.

"I didn't date much," she said. "Too tall. Too fat. Too shy. Then Dad fixed me up with the son of the guy whose company is Good Hands' biggest corporate donor."

I wondered if she meant Strickland Architecture and Chaz Strickland.

She turned a tragic face to me. "What if Good Hands loses all that money because of me?"

"Because of you? Bailey, there were two of you involved. Why should the father withdraw the money when his son harmed you so badly?" I made a disgusted sound. "If anything he should up the ante as some sort of compensation. But that's beside the point. I want to hear the rest of your story."

She sighed. "It's not very pretty. In fact it's sort of pathetic. I'm pathetic. When I knew we were going out, I was thrilled because Chaz is this good-looking guy. I felt grateful that he was willing to spend time with me and be seen with me. Honored like if a king gives a peasant a coin or a kind person pets a lost pup. Pretty pitiful, huh?"

She looked at me, her face a mask of self-loathing and pain.

"We went to the movies. I was so shy I could hardly talk to him, but he didn't seem to care. Then after the movie he didn't drive me home. Instead he pulled into this narrow road by a cornfield and parked."

Oh, kiddo. An old, old story made unique only by the personal pain of each girl hurt.

"I should have said, 'Take me home.' I should have said, 'No!' But he was so handsome and I was so not pretty. When he kissed me, there I was, feeling grateful again. Grateful! Then he was doing more than he should and I knew that I had to stop him, but I swear I didn't know it could happen so fast. I thought it would just be all slow and romantic with lots of time to cut things off. I'd always dreamed of moonlight and roses, and violins and true love, you know? What I got was yuck! Get away from me! What have you done?" She shuddered at the memories.

I thought of Curt and how much I was looking forward to our being one. "When it's the right time and the right person, it will be all those wonderful things, Bailey."

She shrugged. Obviously she didn't believe me, but maybe that was good for the time being. She could sort it all out in coming years.

"Not that it matters," she said. "I've screwed up my life for good."

"Well, I agree you've put a crimp in it, and plan A—high school, college, marriage as a virgin—has gone out the window. But plan B can be wonderful, too. Just different."

"But God has a plan for our lives and I blew mine." She sounded so defeated.

"Come on, Bailey." I made my voice brusque. "One misstep and God's hands are tied? You know better than that. We're talking God here. He's so much bigger than we could ever imagine. He's creative. He's full of possibilities. He's not limited in any way, even by our mistakes and wrongdoings. He makes the evil that men do turn out for good, Genesis says. He can take your current mess and work wonders from it for you if you trust Him. Plan B, Bailey. Plan B. It can be every bit as exciting and fulfilling as plan A. Just different."

TWENTY-FOUR

When Elise started to whimper and her little mouth began moving, I knew it was feeding time. It was also time for me to go. I kissed both girls goodbye and went to join Curt, who was watching a baseball game on the silent TV in the waiting room.

We rode the elevator down and were walking across the lobby when Tug and Candy came through the doors, arms loaded with brightly wrapped gifts. Their own private baby shower? Candy thrust her armload into Tug's already burdened arms and rushed me. She hugged me fiercely.

"Thank you! Thank you so much," she whispered. She pulled back, her eyes shiny with tears. "I don't know how we're going to handle all this yet, but we'll manage."

Tug nodded. "She's a great kid. She really is." His tone was urgent, as if he were pressing an opinion he doubted others agreed with.

"You don't have to convince us," I said. "We know."

"It breaks my heart that she put herself through this

alone." A single tear slid down Candy's cheek, somehow more heartbreaking than a lachrymose flood. "I suspected she was pregnant, but every time I broached the topic, she always said, 'Mom, how could you think such a thing?' Never a direct answer or a direct lie. And because I didn't want it to be true, I didn't press."

Poor Bailey, I thought, being careful of the letter of the law after she'd broken one of the Big Ten. "She thought she was protecting you and Good Hands."

Tug closed his eyes as if in pain. "I'd give up Good Hands in a minute if it would make things better for her. Doesn't she know that?"

"Sort of," I said. "She doesn't doubt your love, but she needs to hear over and over again how much you value her because right now she doesn't value herself at all."

We talked for a few more minutes, then Curt and I left.

"Boy, life can be hard sometimes," I said as I climbed into Curt's car. "Complicated."

He slid behind the wheel. "Are you talking about the Mercers or yourself?"

A puff of air escaped as I saw what he meant. "I guess things are a bit weird for us, too. So let's do what all good Americans do when things are tough. Let's go shopping so I'll at least have some clean underwear for tomorrow."

We spent the rest of the day shopping for clothes to replace all those lost in the explosion and fire. We spent a frustrating evening filling out paperwork for insurance claims, license and credit card replacements, and all the other little things that have to be done after loss.

Monday I got to work bright and early with Doug as

my chaperone and wrote a piece about Ken Mackey showing up Saturday night. I called his parents' house and got him out of bed for a quote.

"Martha was great, especially to me," he said. "I loved her because she stood by me when I got out of jail, when lots of other people wouldn't give me the time of day. There aren't many really kind people in this world and it is beyond sad that we have lost her." He cleared his throat. "When they find him, I hope they hang him from the nearest lamppost. Uh, that last is not for publication." And he hung up.

I'd barely sent my material to Mac for his edit and approval when the phone rang again.

"Merry Kramer," I said into the receiver.

"This is Esther Colby."

Martha's mother!

"I told this to the police and I'm telling it to you. I want you to put it in your paper to help us catch—" Her voice broke.

"I'm very sorry for your loss, Mrs. Colby," I said into the emotionally fraught silence.

"Thanks," she mumbled. "What's so sad is that I just found her after all these years. Not that she'd gone anywhere, but I finally got smart enough to look her up. We'd been e-mailing back and forth for a couple of years now."

I wondered if Steve and Nanette Colby knew and if they were bothered or pleased by Esther's sudden reappearance in Martha's life.

"I decided to come and see her," Esther continued. "Up until now I thought it was better for her and less complicated for me if I remained on the edge of her life, but then she started talking about this wonderful new guy she was going with, this Mac. But there was something about the way she wrote about him sometimes, that made me edgy. I'd married the wrong guy for me, and I didn't want her to make the same mistake. Of course, Steve is basically nice, just dull, dull, dull. Martha's guy sounded—" Esther hesitated "—dangerous, I guess. That sounds extreme, but that's how I felt. Dull's bad enough. Dangerous is a whole different ball game. So I came."

She fell silent. I waited for a minute, then asked, "Did you get to see her?"

She cleared her throat. "I did. Twice. I asked her point-blank about this guy. Was he hurting her? Physically, I mean."

"Was he?"

"She tried to deny it, but her lip hadn't healed from where he'd slugged her. And you know why? Because he found out she'd told me about him. It was supposed to be some sort of a special, secret romance. Give me a break."

"Couldn't have been too special to him if he didn't want anyone to know," I said.

"Tell me about it. He was just using her and she was too blind to see it. But she kept saying she loved him. She'd change him. She knew she would. Look at how Ken had changed. I tried to tell her that Ken had just grown up, seen how stupid it was to keep breaking the law. He'd never hurt her or anyone else."

"Did you ever meet this new man?" I doubted she

had for two reasons. One, it was a "secret" romance. And two, no one was trying to blow her up. Of course, I hadn't seen him, either, and someone was still trying to blow me up.

"No, I never met him. But I want you to write about him. I want you to warn girls about men like him. I want you to save their lives. I want you to save nice people like Martha's father and stepmother and her sisters from having broken hearts. I gotta leave town—can't stand Amhearst. Gives me the creeps. I feel like I'm suffocating here—but you write about him, you hear?"

"I hear. Can I ask you a couple of questions?"

"About Martha?"

"Yes. Mrs. Wilson, her neighbor, says that there were two people at her condo the morning she was killed. One was the new boyfriend."

"Mac."

"Right. Mrs. Wilson thought the other was Ken, but we now know he wasn't even in the state, let alone in Amhearst on that date. Do you have any idea who it might have been?"

"You mean, was it me? 'Cause it wasn't. Not that I can prove it, but it wasn't."

"Okay. Second question—do you have any idea where this Mac lived or what he did for a job?"

"I wish I did, but I don't. I don't think Martha was ever at his place. He always came to hers. And she never mentioned his work to me. Probably afraid he'd slug her again."

"Thank you, Mrs. Colby. Call me if you think of anything, okay?"

When she had hung up, I leaned back in my chair and thought about nice men and terrible men. Lots of times a terrible man was easy to spot, but lots of times he hid behind a nice-guy facade until some unfortunate woman was caught in his web. How could a young girl like Bailey spot a Chaz in time to save herself? Or a trusting, kind woman like Martha see a Mac for what he was? How were you guaranteed a Curt or a Doug Reeder or—I glanced toward the big picture window and the man seated there—or a Mac Carnuccio?

Well, if I ever figured that out, I could write a book called *Ten Ways to Spot a Good Guy Guaranteed* and retire a millionaire.

I got up and went to talk to Mac about how to make use of my serendipitous interview with Esther Colby. The paper had been put to bed for today, so whatever he decided, I had plenty of time to play with the material.

"So how did your visit with the Mercer kid go yesterday?" he asked before I even had a chance to tell him about Esther.

"Pretty well. She feels crummy, of course, both physically and emotionally, but she's a good kid. Given time and some good help and sound counsel, she should be okay."

"Sit." He pointed to the chair I'd sat in for the first time on Friday.

"Two workdays in a row? Be careful. Precedent being set."

"Skip the sarcasm and sit."

I did.

"I've been thinking about that baby all weekend," he said. "It brought back all kinds of memories of my older sister, Giavanna. She had a baby when she was seventeen. Little Angela. Of course, Angie's twenty now and we all love her like crazy. But back when Gia was carrying her—" He shook his head.

"It was bad. My parents wanted her to marry the father, but Gia refused. 'I made one mistake,' she said. 'Don't ask me to make another.' The guy solved the problem by disappearing and not returning to Amhearst for three years. Turns out he had enlisted and sworn his parents to secrecy."

Mac started straightening a pile of papers, a sure sign he was agitated. He never straightened his papers. His hands finally stilled and he started talking again.

"I was only ten and the arguments scared me. I'd lie in bed and listen to Mom and Dad reaming Gia out for embarrassing the family, for having no standards, for being loose. She'd yell right back that she was not an embarrassment, she had standards, she wanted this baby and they'd better get used to it. But I'd hear her crying in her room in the middle of the night. It was a long time before they forgave each other for all the terrible things they had yelled."

I could set his mind at ease about one thing, anyway. "Tug and Candy are standing behind Bailey. They'll do everything they can to help her."

"If she keeps the baby, they'll need to. Wonderful as little Angie was, she brought Gia's life as she knew it to an abrupt halt, especially her social life. Boys suddenly saw her as either fast and easy or as a mom with a kid. The first group she didn't want. She wasn't dumb enough to get stung twice. The second group didn't want her. Even into her midtwenties guys would take her out once or twice, but when they found out about Angie, they disappeared. Gia was twenty-seven when Bob came around. He was thirty, old enough to deal with having a kid that wasn't his." Mac smiled. "He was the best thing that ever happened to the two of them."

"They have their own kids?" I was fascinated by this slice of Mac's life. All I'd ever heard him talk about before was his mother and her distress that he didn't go to church. Of course, Dawn was changing that even if it wasn't the church Mrs. Carnuccio would have preferred.

"They've got three great guys."

I grinned. Proud Uncle Mac.

He reached back and whipped out his wallet. I saw a picture of three little boys with dark hair and dark eyes and mischief as obvious on their faces as a sprinkling of freckles would have been. He flipped the photo holder and there was a gorgeous dark-haired young woman.

"Angie? She's beautiful."

Mac nodded. "She was probably ten or twelve before Mom and Gia really forgave each other for that terrible time and terrible words. 'Of course I forgive you, Gia,' Mom would say for years, 'but if you ever do something like that again…' She sounded like that was exactly what she expected Gia to do. Or if Gia was late coming home, 'What was his name, Gia? And what did you do that you're so late, as if I didn't know?' Or, my favorite, 'What do you think, Gia? Can a leopard change his spots? Can a bad girl ever be anything but a bad girl?'"

"Yikes. Poor Gia."

"I know Mom was scared and a lot of her fear came out in anger, but understanding that didn't make things any easier for Gia. Bailey's parents—they need to forgive her and not let the resentment over the forced changes in their lives fester for years. And that means they can't bring it up every time they get mad at her over something. If there's one thing that I've learned, it's that forgiveness, true forgiveness, means gone."

I studied him for a few seconds, thinking what a mixture of wisdom and hardheadedness he was.

"What?" he demanded. "Did I say something wrong?"

I spoke carefully because I thought we were on very important ground here. "Given Gia's story, I understand why you're so concerned for Bailey and I understand why you see forgiveness as so important between her and her parents. But, Mac, what I don't understand is why you have so much trouble with forgiveness when it relates to you. Why can't you see that you can be forgiven?"

He narrowed his eyes. "We are not talking about me."

"Yes, we are. Mac, don't you see? You want everybody to forgive everybody, but you won't let people or God forgive you. Doesn't that sound a bit strange? Or contradictory?"

"Drop it, Merry."

I ignored him. Sometimes things just needed saying.

"The very thing you want others to offer and receive, you refuse to receive. For some reason you seem to think you're too bad to be forgiven. It's like God looks at you and says, 'Oh, I can't handle Carnuccio. He's too much for me.' Or Jesus says, 'I died for everyone but Carnuccio. He's beyond my power to save.' Right? It's like you're telling God, 'Thanks, but no thanks.'"

"Merry, you're meddling." His voice was as cold as a refrigerated meat locker. "No one talks to me like that but Dawn."

"Well, as of now, me, too." I leaned forward in my chair. *Dear Lord, let him hear me.* "Mac, in a sense it doesn't matter what you've done in your past. The Lord wants to forgive you for any and all of it. Jesus became our great guilt bearer when He died on that blood-stained cross. It may sound clichéd that all you need to do is believe in Jesus and be saved, be forgiven. But like many clichés, it's the truth."

"Thank you, Reverend Merry."

I should have felt flash-frozen, but I didn't. "That nasty attitude of yours used to work," I said as I stood, knowing it was time to leave. "But that was back before I realized you were a chocolate-covered cherry." I smiled. "Just do me one favor. Think about what you're telling God when you say you're too bad to be forgiven. Think about what that says about the great sacrifice Jesus made for you. Do you really want to say no thanks?"

He glared at me.

"I'm going right now," I assured him and fled to my desk. We could talk about Esther Colby later.

At lunchtime Jolene and Edie walked to Ferretti's with me, keeping so close in their effort to protect me that it was all I could do not to trip over them.

"How come this guy isn't trying to get me?" Jo asked as we slid into our booth. She looked slightly put out that she was being left out. "I'm the one who tripped over Martha's foot."

I'd voiced the same question to Mac, but since I had no more answer today than when I'd originally asked, I merely shrugged. Edie looked at her as though she was a few rhinestones short of a necklace.

"It's a fair question," Jo shot back, just a tad defensive.

"Read the menu, Jolene," Edie ordered. "I'll contact the demolition guys after we get back to the office and get your bomb ticking."

Jo gave her a sour smile, but she did get busy considering her order and forgot the questions.

Later that afternoon when it was time for me to go see Tony Compton, Jolene offered to walk me down the street.

I politely declined. "I'm walking a few doors down on Main Street. What can possibly happen?"

Mr. Weldon was in the front hall up in his stepladder changing a ceiling lightbulb when I arrived unscathed. Of course, I'd spent the three-minute walk looking over my shoulder every ten seconds, but who's telling?

"Merry," he said as he saw me. "I need to talk to you!"

I was in no humor to hear more slander about Mac. I smiled vaguely up at him. "I can't stop right now. I've got an appointment." I hurried to the stairs.

"Well, I'll look for you when you leave. It's important," he called after me.

I just bet. More bash-Mac stuff.

I walked into the reception area of the law firm. Annie was wearing a skirt again today and it reminded me of the article idea on dressing for work that I needed to pitch to Mac.

"Mr. Compton is expecting you," she said. "Just knock."

I knocked, pleased that today I didn't have to wait around for Tony to return from court. His deep voice called, "Come in."

He rose to greet me, his smile going full bore. "It's so good to see you again!" Like it had been years. He shook my hand and ushered me to the chairs before his desk, but I was too busy looking around the office to sit.

There was no sign of all the boxes and clutter of his moving in. Impressive legal tomes and reference books lined the shelves. Awards and diplomas hung on the walls or sat in strategic breaks on the shelves. A file cabinet fronted with wood sat along the far wall beside a closet. And my handprint had disappeared.

"Very nice," I said. "Someone's been working hard."

"Annie," Tony said, smiling that charming smile. "She unpacked it all. I just put the books on the shelves where I wanted them."

On the edge of his desk sat a very healthy philodendron; a flourishing ficus tree stood by the window. I indicated them with my hand. "Annie?"

"Annie."

A pair of signed baseballs sat on little stands on the corner of the filing cabinet. I walked over and saw Cal Ripkin Jr.'s autograph on both. Next to them was a black Baltimore Orioles cap with an orange oriole embroidered on it, and leaning against the cabinet was a baseball bat, also autographed. On the wall beside the filing cabinet was a shadow box holding a baseball jersey bearing the legandary orange number 8 and the same autograph.

"Not from Annie, I trust?"

He shook his head. "Never. I got them on a couple of my many trips to Camden Yards. Caught that ball when Cal hit a foul." He pointed to the one on the left. "I got the shirt right off Cal's back at a charity auction night."

I was impressed. Even I knew about the legendary and now-retired Ripkin, one of the good guys of baseball.

"I got the other ball at a baseball card show where Cal was autographing. I got the bat on eBay. Four of my proudest possessions. There was never anyone like Cal."

The way he said Cal, you'd have thought they were best personal buds, but that's the way it was with true fans. They did feel like best buds with whomever they idolized.

I walked back to the chairs by Tony's desk and sat. My eye fell on the fancy metal name plaque sitting on his desk. M. Anthony Compton, Esq. "Annie?"

He frowned and shook his head. "My mom. Law school graduation. But Annie put it there."

"Ah. And the *M* stands for?"

He tried to force a smile, but something had angered him. Hadn't I fawned over his Ripkin trophies enough? "Michael."

Michael Anthony Compton.

My breath hitched.

MAC.

TWENTY-FIVE

Mac? Tony?

Words from Martha's diary raced through my mind: No wonder he can convince people so well. Words are his stock in trade.

They didn't have to refer to an editor as some seemed to think. They could refer to a lawyer just as readily.

Then another memory popped up and I felt my skin grow chilled.

"He always wears a cap with some logo on it," Mrs. Wilson had said of the new boyfriend. "It was a bird."

Since we were in suburban Philadelphia, I'd automatically equated bird with eagle, picturing the stylized eagle's-head logo of the city's football franchise. But Tony had lived in Harrisburg, right up the interstate from Baltimore. And I'd never asked Mrs. Wilson what color the bird was, only the cap. I was willing to bet that the bird was orange, an orange oriole just like the one stitched on the black cap sitting on the file cabinet. Oriole, not eagle. Baseball, not football.

I bent quickly to pull my camera out of my purse. I

didn't want Tony to see my face since everyone said that what I was thinking showed there clearly. I needed a few seconds to wipe all expression away.

But my mind kept churning. What possible motive could he have for killing Martha? By all accounts she was as threatening as a newborn pup.

Well, for one thing, if it came out he was beating on her, there went his career and his reputation. I wondered suddenly about Valerie Gladstone, his dead fiancée. Had he been abusive to her? I made a mental note to contact the Harrisburg police and Representative Gladstone, Valerie's father. My blood started to fizz as I contemplated the story I might be about to break.

Easy, kid. You're jumping to conclusions—big ones.

My new mini-tape recorder tumbled out of my purse as I rooted for the new little camera I'd gotten to replace the one that had been in my old purse in the car. So did my new cell phone. I grabbed the phone and slid it back in the pocket in the lining I'd designated as its home. Unfortunately the soft-sided purse I had just bought was always collapsing and the phone was always sliding free. I grabbed the little recorder, too. Then, face as bland as I could manage, I straightened, giving him a small smile, trying not to fidget as he studied me.

"Where do you want to stand for your picture?" I asked brightly. I sounded very false to my ears and I fretted that he heard the same phony tone.

He blinked and broke his stare, then gestured behind him. "I thought I could stand by the bookshelves with an open book in my hand, like I'm researching something, you know?"

"Good idea," I said, trying not to remember that someone had destroyed my car and my apartment and this man might be the one who had done it. "Different from the static head shot." And, I couldn't help thinking, it keeps a full face shot from being in the paper to be recognized by someone like Mrs. Wilson.

Tony walked over and stood by a shelf lined with legal references in matching bindings. He pulled one down and opened it.

I looked through my viewfinder. The light from the window fell across him, creating interesting light and shadow contrast. I also saw the clenched jaw and tense shoulders of an angry man.

Didn't killers usually follow the same pattern in their crimes? Snipers stayed snipers. Stranglers stayed stranglers. If Tony did kill Martha with that rock, then what about the bombs for me?

A new thought made the hair on the back of my neck stand up. What about Valerie Gladstone, his dead fiancée? Could Tony have killed her? Again the question was why. Perhaps he had roughed her up as he had Martha. Perhaps she called him on it or was going to tell people and in a fury he killed her.

Perhaps I've read too many mystery novels.

"Relax," I said to him even as I tried to take the word to heart myself. The last thing I wanted was for my nervousness and suspicions to be obvious to him. "Smile."

He gave a reasonable facsimile of his usual smile and I took several shots. "Turn a little toward me. Look up. That's good." I clicked away like I had nothing on my mind but making him look good.

Could Mrs. Wilson pick him out in a lineup? Very questionable with the baseball cap and the evening visits to impede her view of him. Even if she did identify him, a good defense lawyer would make a big deal of her age and eyesight.

I thought of all the times I'd felt uncomfortable around Tony. I'd thought it was because he came on too strong. Had it been because he somehow gave off evil vibes?

Get a grip, Merry!

"How did things work out Saturday night with Ken Mackey at the police station?" I asked. After all, I was a reporter, so I'd better ask questions and this one seemed safe enough. He'd seen me there, even talked to me. "Did his statement check out?"

"It did." The answer was clipped, almost snarled.

"It would be an easy alibi to verify," I said as I snapped away. I walked around the desk so I was facing him head-on. Snap. Snap. "Not like some."

"Like Carnuccio?"

I hadn't been thinking of anyone or anything in particular when I made that comment. I was just talking to fill the time until I could get myself safely out of here, but I bristled at his Mac comment. Here was one too many people jumping on a man I liked and admired and I became defensive before I thought.

"Don't say things like that about Mac, Tony. He's a good man and I don't believe he had anything to do with Martha's death." I heard myself and ordered, *Shut up, woman!*

Tony closed the book in his hand and slid it into its

place on the shelf. "Your loyalty is commendable, if misdirected."

I gave a tight smile of acknowledgment. "Well, I think that does it," I said as I took a step toward my purse. "I've got everything I need."

"Really?" Tony said as he walked around the desk toward me. "I thought we were going to do some more interview stuff." He picked up his name plaque and began fiddling with it, his fingers running over the inscribed letters. He glanced down as if checking that they hadn't changed.

"I've got more than enough," I said, forcing my eyes away from the plaque. "And if I have any questions, I'll just give you a call." I shoved my camera in my purse.

When he looked up from the plaque, his eyes were cold and flat. I shivered.

"Thanks for your time, Tony." I turned and practically ran to the door. I was reaching for the knob when Tony, alarmingly close, said, "I knew you'd be trouble. I knew it." He sounded almost regretful. Almost.

Then he brought the plaque down on my head with appalling power.

TWENTY-SIX

I don't know how long I was out, but when I woke up it was dark. My head throbbed, and I felt nauseated. I was curled on my side, knees drawn up, on a hard surface and I had no idea where I was or how I had gotten there. I tried to sit up, but had to stop moving immediately because my stomach screamed, "No!" and a cold sweat broke out all over my body. I lay still and swallowed repeatedly.

When I thought I wasn't going to throw up after all, I brought up a hand to hold my head on my shoulders since it felt ready to fall off. My knuckles slammed into another hard surface. That's when I discovered that I was in a small, cramped area, and every horror movie I'd ever been foolish enough to watch told me I'd been buried alive.

I moved my hand around and felt surfaces on four sides and below me, but there was open space above. Taking a deep breath, I slowly, slowly pushed myself into a sitting position. For a few minutes I just sat, eyes closed, resting my head against the wall behind me. How could I be so tired and sick?

When I opened my eyes, the nausea wasn't as bad as it had been, an encouraging fact. I ran my hands over the four surfaces that hemmed me in, and it was the indentations on the fourth surface that told me where I was. I was in a closet, and the uneven surface was the inside to a door done in the traditional cross and Bible design.

Where there was a door, there was a knob.

I reached eagerly for it, only to pull back at the last minute. Whoever had put me here might be just the other side. Did I want to see him? Maybe I could look under the door and see if I was alone or not.

Again moving very slowly, I got to my knees and bent. My mouth filled with saliva and once again I battled intense vertigo. I stayed still with my forehead resting on the floor until I felt it safe to move again.

I turned and rested the side of my face against the floor and peered under the door. All I could see were floorboards and the edge of a light-colored rug. As I sat again, I struggled to remember.

The floor vibrated under heavy footfalls and I pushed back as far from the door as I could, which wasn't far at all. But the footsteps didn't stop at the closet. Instead I heard another door open and a man say in a raised voice, "Thanks for your time, Merry. See you later." Then the door shut again and the footfalls passed the closet again.

The sound of the voice clicked on my memory. M. Anthony Compton. MAC, not Mac. He'd hit me! I felt outrage, a foolish emotion when I had been shoved in a closet and was being held here.

And what was with the see-you-later-Merry bit? It

must have been for the benefit of the others in the office, Mr. Grassley and Mr. Jordan and the skirted Annie. The two men might be in their own offices, but Annie would see that I hadn't left. She'd know something was wrong. Unless she wasn't there to see?

In the total silence that lingered outside my door, I heard the faint opening of a far door and the last gurgle of a flushed toilet. I was willing to bet Annie had been using the restroom and that Tony had been waiting for just that moment for me to "leave."

I heard a loud tap on glass.

"Yes?" Tony said.

"I'm leaving, Mr. Compton," Annie called. "Mr. Grassley and Mr. Jordan have left already. Can I get you anything before I go?"

"Thank you, Annie, but no. Have a good evening." He sounded so nice and friendly.

Just as I opened my mouth to scream to catch Annie's attention before she left, the door to the closet flew open.

"Don't even think about it," Tony muttered at me, a baseball bat held over his head. He brought it swinging down. For a split second I was so shocked I couldn't move. Then I dodged as much as I could in the confines of the closet. The bat caught me on the edge of my right shoulder, sending pain streaking down my arm and across my back.

I gasped and stared at him, incredulous. People didn't hit people with baseball bats, not people I knew. I'd spent time with this man. He and I had had dinner together. He'd walked me to my car and kissed my red palm. He'd flirted with me!

And now he thought he'd disabled me. Somehow in all the time we'd spent with him talking and me writing, he hadn't noticed I was left-handed.

"I knew you were trouble as soon as I realized you were the woman with the diary," he said through gritted teeth, his face a mask of dislike. "I knew it was only a matter of time before you figured everything out."

I didn't like cowering on the floor as he towered over me. It was bad enough he had a normal height and weight advantage, but I didn't need to let him dominate me as he so clearly wanted to. I forced myself to my feet, holding my injured shoulder, fighting off lingering dizziness from the hit on the head. I was still in the closet, still his prisoner, but at least I was upright. "How do you know I found the diary?"

"I saw you."

I heard once again the swish that had made me think of the sliding door and screen being moved. "You were inside when I got there."

He nodded. "I went out the back and didn't realize I'd dropped the diary until I got to my car. Then I hid behind the evergreens out back, waiting for you to leave."

"You were there watching?" I felt creepy all over, like little spiders were crawling on me, all but my right arm, which felt numb. I thought you always felt when someone was watching you, but obviously you didn't.

"I was there. I saw you come outside and pick up the book. I watched you put it in your purse when that nosy old lady next door came out. Then she chased you with that burglar bar."

For a moment, the fury in his face abated and he

actually smiled. "I don't think I've ever seen anything so funny as you running from that old woman." He threw back his head and laughed.

Happy to entertain you, I thought sourly. I took advantage of his looking away to try and assess my chances of getting past him and to the door. They weren't very high.

He sobered quickly and stared at me. "And then you showed up to interview me."

A thought flashed through my mind. "You walked me to my car to see what I drove, didn't you? So you could blow it up."

He stared at me, malevolence oozing from every pore. "The car wasn't my target."

Like I needed the reminder. "And the house. You fixed that, too, didn't you?"

"I timed it to twenty seconds after you opened the door. Time for you to get inside, but not time for you to notice anything wrong."

"But Whiskers got out and saved the day. He made me cautious. When I saw the broken glass and smelled the accelerant, I never really went inside."

"Pity. It would have been easier on us both."

I forced myself not to show him the terror that comment induced. "I thought killers used the same modus operandi all the time."

"First, I'm not a killer."

"What?"

"A killer plans and premeditates. Martha was an accident. And it was her fault."

"It was her fault you hit her hard enough with a rock to kill her?"

"She was threatening me. She was going to tell about our relationship."

"She was going to tell about the abuse."

"It wasn't abuse. She always asked for whatever she got."

"Telling her mother about you asked for a broken tooth?"

"She was misrepresenting me to her mother. I did not deserve what she planned to do. She was going to tell Grassley and Jordan."

Amazing to me how he excused himself and made Martha the one in the wrong. "So Martha might have been spontaneous." If you counted having a murderous rock in hand at a deserted spot at a very early hour as spontaneous. "But trying to kill me was premeditated."

"Self-defense," he said, and it was obvious he'd convinced himself that was true.

"So," I asked, trying to seem much braver than I felt, "what are you going to do with me this time?"

He gave a tight smile. "Throws them off, all the different methods."

"Knife. Rock. Explosives. Baseball bat?"

He shrugged. "You'll find out soon enough."

He hadn't even blinked at the word knife. Poor Valerie Gladstone.

"Everyone knows I'm here," I said.

"Were here," he corrected. "Annie heard me saying goodbye. You left a good ten minutes ago."

Just like I'd thought. *Lord, how do we trip him up?*

I glanced at the window. From this angle all I could see was an apartment across the street and its curtains were pulled tight. But Main Street was down there one story and Main Street meant people and people meant help.

"Be right back," Tony said suddenly and walked out of the room.

I ran to the window. It was tall, and I had to stretch to reach the latch to unlock the sash. I grabbed the window pulls and yanked. Pain shrieked up my right arm, and I realized that the window was too heavy to lift even if my arm had been strong.

If you can't pull, push. I reached up and put my palms against the glass below the upper sash and shoved. Nothing. I pushed again, desperate. I felt the sash move. I readied myself for another push when an arm snaked about my waist and I was lifted off my feet.

"No, no, no," Tony insisted. "Mustn't draw any attention. Someone else might get hurt, you know."

With a quick thrust of his hip and shove from his hand, he tossed me across the room. I landed against the bookshelves, each shelf digging into my back as I slid to the floor. Blinking against the shooting pain in my injured shoulder, I leaped to my feet.

"Don't you touch me again!" Brave, empty words to a man once again swinging his baseball bat.

He moved another couple of steps toward me as I struggled to my feet.

"You can't kill me with that bat." Much to my disgust my voice was trembling. "You'll get blood all over the office. It might not show on the walls, but it'll definitely stain the rug."

"I don't plan to kill you with the bat, though it would give me great satisfaction to swing at you like I'd swing for the fences. All I plan to do is knock you out."

"Just try it," I challenged. "I won't be taken unawares this time. But let's just say you succeed. Then what?"

He glanced at the pillow he'd gotten from the chairs in the waiting area in the reception room. Once such a pillow had made me comfortable as I waited for that first interview.

"You're going to knock me out, then smother me?" The man was seriously deranged.

He began moving toward me, slapping the bat against his palm. As he started around the desk, I started moving around it, too. Maybe we could play circle the desk until I came up with an idea to save myself, something short of flinging myself out a closed window thirty or so feet above concrete.

I wasn't prepared for him to launch himself across the desk and grab my wrist. I screamed without thought and began flailing wildly as I struggled to escape. He tightened his grip and began to twist my arm.

"No!" I grabbed the first thing that came to hand, the M. Anthony Compton name plaque. I swung indiscriminately at his arm, at his body extended over the desk, whacking him again and again. With a growl he released my wrist and hauled himself across the desk. I backed away until I was up against the file cabinet.

I still had the nameplate in my hand, but he had both longer arms and a baseball bat.

"Dear God, help!"

"Nobody's going to help you, sweetheart," Tony said, his face scarily devoid of all expression, even anger. He took one slow step, then another, the bat resting on his shoulder. I pressed into the wall, wishing I could push through it into the adjoining room.

As I glanced with longing at the window, I saw white out of the corner of my eye. I spun and grabbed one of Tony's precious Cal Ripkin baseballs. I drew back my left arm and threw it at the window with everything I had.

The glass shattered as the ball sailed through. As I began to scream and scream and scream, I prayed the glass didn't fall on anyone or the ball bean anyone. Then I grabbed the second ball and threw it at Tony, who stood staring in disbelief at the shattered window.

I wanted to hit him in the side of the head and maybe knock him unconscious, but at the last second he turned to me and the ball got him square in the nose. He bellowed in pain as blood spurted. He grabbed his face and went to his knees.

I ran forward and grabbed the forgotten bat and threw it into the closet. I bent and snatched my mini recorder from its resting place beside the leg of Tony's desk where I'd left it when everything fell out of my bag.

Gripping it tightly, I raced into the reception room and reached for the office doorknob just as the door burst open. I found myself running into Curt's open arms as he and Mr. Weldon burst into the office. Behind them, William Poole lumbered up the stairs.

TWENTY-SEVEN

That evening as Curt and I drove to Jolene and Reilly's for a late dinner, I wanted to tell him something that had been in the back of my head ever since I saw Tony swing that bat at me. I'd just needed some time for the thought to percolate through the exhilaration of survival and the business of making statements.

I took a breath, but before I could say anything, he grabbed my hand and, eyes still on the road, said, "I've been thinking about something, sweetheart."

I knew from his tone that whatever it was was serious. I braced myself.

"When I heard you screaming and thought I might lose you—" He swallowed. "The possibility still makes me break into a cold sweat."

"Tell me about it," I said, my voice wary.

He gave a brief smile. "Anyway, it hit me how stupid I was being about where we were going to live. Anywhere with you would be wonderful, if nerve-racking upon occasion."

I squeezed his hand. "I was—"

"No," he interrupted. "Let me finish." He took a deep breath and swallowed. "I think it would be nice if we lived in Pittsburgh. You'll enjoy your family and you were right. I can paint anywhere. While you were talking to William, I called the West Carolina Art Institute and told them I wasn't interested."

I stared at him. "You didn't!" I felt the tears gather. "I think that's the nicest thing anyone has ever done for me!"

He turned and gave me a quick grin. "I can love you wherever we live and you're what counts. When I thought I might lose you, I realized that if I really loved you, I'd want you to be happy."

"Even if you're not?"

"But that's what I realized. It's you, not the place and not the job."

"I love you." I lifted his hand and kissed his knuckles. "But we can't live in Pittsburgh."

He shot me a quick glance. "Why not?"

"While you were in the men's room at the police station, I called Mr. Henrey and told him no to the *Chronicle*'s offer. When I thought Tony might do me in, I realized that wherever I was, if I was with you, that's what counted and if you wanted to live in North Carolina, so did I."

We pulled up in front of Jo's and Curt turned off the motor. He turned to me and we just looked at each other.

"'The Gift of the Magi,'" I said. "Carlyle-Kramer style."

We were enjoying a pretty scorching kiss when there was a knock on my window.

"Save it for later," Jo called. "We're waiting for you."

I knew I was still blushing when we walked into her lovely home. Reilly was standing in the entry hall.

"I told her to wait," he said, "but she insisted on rushing out." He looked at his wife with affectionate exasperation. "You know Jolene."

"Come on into the living room and sit for a few minutes," Jo said, leading the way.

I was looking over my shoulder, grinning at Curt as we entered the room, and was completely surprised when several people yelled, "Surprise!"

I jumped and stared at the roomful of friends. Maddie and Doug. Dawn and Mac, Mac looking like a weight had been rolled off his back. Edie and her husband, Tom. Mr. and Mrs. Weldon. Even Larry the sports guy and his wife, Lori. And in front of the love seat was a great pile of gifts.

"It's a his and hers shower." Jo showed us to our seats.

"Do we still get dinner?" Curt asked.

"After the presents," she said. "In the meantime, nibble on the hors d'oeuvres."

Quite frankly, I love presents, so I had a great time opening my half. Curt seemed both embarrassed and pleased to open his—mostly unexciting things like tools.

As I looked around the room at these people who had become so dear to me, I wondered how I could have thought to leave them. I leaned to Curt and whispered that thought.

"I was just thinking the same thing." He tore the

paper off what proved to be a pair of red boxers with white hearts all over. While everyone hooted, he said, "We're Amhearst through and through, sweetheart."

"Me, too? I'm no longer an outlander?"

"You're an in-lander, if there is such a word."

I let the joy of the evening wash over me, dissipating the lingering horror of my afternoon. Things didn't get much better than this.

As all of us were walking to the dinner table, Mr. Weldon sidled up to me. "Merry, I'm so glad you are all right! I kept waiting for you to come out of Compton's office to tell you I figured out who was saying those terrible things about Mac Carnuccio."

I knew now that he'd gotten so worried about how long I was with Tony Compton that he called Curt, who called William. It turned out that William, having figured out the MAC, was already suspicious of Tony, and had been talking with the Harrisburg police about the death of Valerie Gladstone. Curt and William rushed to the office building and arrived just as the ball sailed through the window, landing on the roof of William's patrol car, making a nice dent.

My screams had sent them rushing up the steps.

Standing now in Jo's dining room, Mr. Weldon paused and glanced at Mac, talking with Dawn and the Reeders. "It was Compton who fed me all that stuff, but he was so clever about it. He'd stop me to ask about new lightbulbs or his name on the door and before he left, he'd drop a little something like, 'It must be unnerving to the town to have someone suspected in a crime as the editor of the paper' or 'I heard at the courthouse that the police have a diary with the name *Mac* in it. Makes you wonder, doesn't it?'"

"I'm not surprised, Mr. Weldon. He was trying to turn attention away from himself."

He shook his head. "Well, I'm ashamed I fell for it. You didn't. You were a true friend."

"Well, I know Mac better than you do and I knew he was involved with Dawn. There was no way he was still seeing Martha. Then, too, we've been praying for him to become a Christian."

Mr. Weldon glanced at his wife, busy talking with Jolene. "Mother says we should apologize."

"I think that would be wonderful," I said. "I think offering forgiveness would be good for him right now."

Mr. Weldon nodded and went to get his wife. Together they approached Mac and Dawn. I wished I could hear the conversation, but I saw Mac reach out and shake Mr. Weldon's hand, so I assumed it had gone well.

Dinner was wonderful and the conversation lively, much of it centering around my adventures of the afternoon. Mr. Weldon turned scarlet when everyone made a big thing of his calls to Curt and William.

When it was time to leave, Mac helped Curt carry our gifts to the car. I thanked Jo and Reilly and walked out with Dawn.

"I have news for you, Mac," I said.

"Good news?" He looked at me skeptically, undoubtedly thinking of my *Chronicle* offer.

"I think so. I turned the *Chronicle* down."

"Yes!" He pumped the air. "That's my girl!" He gave me a hug.

"You won't be moving?" Dawn asked.

Curt and I looked at each other and grinned. We shook our heads. And I found I was very satisfied with the thought of staying in Amhearst. This was where we belonged, where our friends were, where our lives were.

"We've got news, too," Dawn said. She looked at Mac.

He looked embarrassed but he said, "I thought more about what you accused me of, Merry."

"What I accused you of?" Wait a minute. I was one of the ones who didn't accuse him.

"I'm not talking about the Martha thing. I'm talking about what I was saying about God and about Jesus' death when I refused to accept the salvation and forgiveness they offered. I'm believing in God for the forgiveness He offers in Jesus."

"Yes!" I threw myself at Mac and hugged him hard. Then I grabbed Dawn.

With this happy news, the week went into overdrive. A new wedding gown arrived all the way from England and Leslie had it ready for me by Friday afternoon. Our rehearsal dinner was great fun and the wedding went off without a hitch, something that surprised me as much as anyone, given the chaos of the previous week.

Saturday night was all I'd dreamed and on Sunday Curt and I flew to Seattle. From there we drove to Olympic National Park where we stayed in a little cabin on a cliff overlooking the Pacific and a beach filled with the trunks of trees washed out to sea and thrown back to collect in stacks higher than our heads.

Monday morning we woke up to look out over the ocean from our bed. We bunched up our pillows and cuddled, watching seagulls dive and soar.

"Happy, sweetheart?" Curt asked.

I smiled into his chest. "I don't think I've ever heard a more foolish question."

"I take it that's a yes?" His arm tightened around me.

"A big yes."

And it was. I had enjoyed the fun and excitement of the wedding and all its associated hoopla, but what I was really looking forward to was our marriage.

"You know," I said as I watched the high tide dash itself upon the countless trunks on the beach, "anyone can have a wedding. A wedding is just an event. An important one, granted, but just an event. A marriage is a life. It only takes money to have a wedding. It takes guts and courage and commitment to have a marriage."

"Well, I know you've got more than your share of those things," my husband whispered in my ear. "Makes me think we've got the future all sewed up."

I raised up on an elbow and looked at him, all rumpled, his beard shadow dark on his face, his breath less than fresh. "If loving were all it took, we'd be guaranteed a happy life, wouldn't we?"

His slow grin made my heart race. "Oh, yes, sweetheart." Then he sobered. "But we both know it takes more than just loving. I promised before God and witnesses to love and care for you always. Let me repeat that vow for your ears alone."

Wow!

"Some day we may end up in Pittsburgh or North Carolina, but wherever we are, Merrileigh Kramer-Carlyle, with the help of God, I will love you as Christ loved the church and gave Himself for her." Then he grinned again. "Your job will be to forgive me when I fail—which I can also promise I will do, though not intentionally, at least not usually."

"Of course I'll forgive you," I said, knowing it would be much harder in the rigors of everyday life than it felt today. "And I promise to do my best to return that same kind of love with respect and appreciation." I stuck a finger in his chest. "Your job will be to accept me when I fail."

"Done," he said, and we settled back to watch the action taking place outside our window, at least until our own action proved more invigorating.

Dear Reader,

We will be attending a retirement celebration for our pastor this evening, and as part of the program, I get to be in front of about five hundred people for about forty-five seconds. Forty-five seconds. I should clarify that. I get to be in front of them for about two minutes, but I get to speak for forty-five seconds. My husband gets the other seventy-five.

We get this honor because when the pastor came to check us out and be checked out—you denominational people don't have to go through this process. Headquarters makes the decision for you—he stayed at our home. We're supposed to tell what we remember from his visit twenty-five years ago.

Like I remember anything he said at the breakfast table twenty-five years ago.

But he had hair back then, and he wore a yellow V-neck sweater, which for some unknown reason I do remember. So I've figured out forty-five seconds' worth of comments that shouldn't embarrass any of us too much.

Now here is my confession: I have spent days agonizing over what to wear, certainly more time than I've devoted to what I'm supposed to say. The red jacket? It's good for catching the eye, but it's not a very warm piece of apparel, and today is a very cold and blustery winter day.

Maybe that cranberry Harris tweed blazer from Talbot's would be better—and warmer. Are blazers too passé? It buttons high, which I think is in, not that I'll be buttoning it. There's something about blazers and women's bodies; they fight with each other constantly, neither ever achieving victory. But hanging open, the tweed should be all right, shouldn't it? At least it's long enough to cover my hips.

I know, I know. The people there will not care what I wear unless I really look awful. They also won't remember a word I say. After all, I don't remember the pastor's words from when he stayed with us all those years ago.

I can't help thinking that I should pay the Lord at least as much attention as I pay the life-altering choice of red jacket or cranberry blazer. I'd certainly be a better person. When the Lord asked Moses, "What is that in your hand?" Moses' reply wasn't, "A cranberry blazer." But then, I don't expect the Lord to turn my blazer into a serpent as he did Moses' staff (Ex. 4).

So what is in my hand? Your hand? The Word of God? My prayer list? Do we have an open-handed policy to care, to comfort, to encourage? If we use our hands in this manner, red jackets and cranberry blazers fade to insignificance while we grow and serve in ways that matter for both time and eternity.

Gayle Roper

QUESTIONS FOR DISCUSSION

1. Curt and Merry both have very good job offers in two different places, not an uncommon thing for today's couples. How do they resolve their problem? How would you resolve such a situation if it happened to you? Say one wants to move because of advancement opportunities and the other can't or won't. Is this grounds for divorce?

2. Mrs. Wilson and Mrs. Anderson are feisty old ladies. What are five things you think a person should do while young to assure a vibrant old age?

3. What do you think of the ethics of Merry going through Martha's house? Where do privacy issues enter into such a scenario?

4. Mac says, "Faith is just optimism by a different name." Do you agree or disagree? What is your rationale? Scriptural support?

5. Tug Mercer says that just repairing people's homes isn't enough. But isn't it better than nothing? What should be added if it isn't enough? What other creative ministries are you familiar with, things that don't involve teaching or preaching, which we see as traditional ministry?

6. What is your reaction to Bailey's keeping her pregnancy a secret? What should she have done? What

does it say about Tug and Candy Mercer that they weren't aware? Was Merry right to take the baby back?

7. If you are married, what do you remember about your engagement period? Why is this so often a tense time? How has today's wedding culture aided or eased the tension?

8. Read Numbers 32:23. Which characters in *Caught Redhanded* are experiencing the truth of this verse? Have you seen this played out in your life? The lives of those you know? What is the ultimate finding out?